The GWEN JOHN SCULPTURE

The
GWEN JOHN
SCULPTURE

John Malcolm

CHARLES SCRIBNER'S SONS
New York

First published in the United States
by Charles Scribner's Sons 1986.

Library of Congress Cataloging-in-Publication Data

Malcolm, John.
  Gwen John sculpture.

  I. Title.
PR6063.A362G9 1986   823'.914   85-22255
ISBN 0-684-18574-1

1 3 5 7 9 11 13 15 17 19 F/C 20 18 16 14 12 10 8 6 4 2

Printed in the United States of America.

CHAPTER 1

Summer morning mist hung grey shrouds over the river as I rattled the car across the bridge at Branne. It gave the swirling waters of the Dordogne a leaden, whorled surface as it ran swiftly beneath me. The French get a lot of morning mist, which may account for their set attitude towards the English weather; they imagine that the further north you travel the more impenetrable it becomes. As I glanced down at the wide expanse of quick-running water, blurred at the edges by the mist, I wondered if the hacked bodies would have floated this far, borne by the current, or whether they would have silted the edges further upstream at Castillon itself and along to the bends at St Jean. The volume looked substantial enough, even now, in June; the idea of trying to ford across on foot seemed absurd, no matter how desperate the need. Not a nice memory, any of it; I shivered as the road turned off the river and I could accelerate away round the right-hand bend towards the junction at St Pey.

Over to my left, about five miles away, St Emilion and the rise in the land that provides the slopes for the better châteaux were hidden by the haze. Here along the river plain the flat land was intensely cultivated and striped with vines, but it could boast of no Château Cheval Blanc or Château Ausone of the distinguished côtes around the town. Good red plonk in Bordeaux bottles is what you would get from here, I thought, as I kept going eastwards, concentrating on the last few minutes to the rendezvous. As the tyres crunched on the odd bits of crisp side-gravel strewn on the road by passing agricultural implements, I kept thinking about Jeremy's indignant words to me on the telephone the night before. He was very steamed up about his uncle's project and had no thought of my convenience. Instant

action was required and I, being in France already, could
be despatched at will from a promising bedroom in a Paris
hotel to the site of what they once called—what was it?—a
dismal fight.

At Castillon-la-Bataille, a few miles on, I had to slow down
and turn off, right, into the middle of the town. I found the
tiny descent that ducks down beside the old stone bridge and
tilted the car's nose to join the lane that runs along the north
bank of the Dordogne like a towpath. The haze was lifting a
bit and the wide river looked less menacing when flanked by
the warm yellow houses and old buildings along its banks.
Early-morning fishermen glanced incuriously at my hired
Renault as I left the town behind, crossing the tiny angled
bridge over the side-stream called the Lidoire before following
the trees along the bank out into the country again. Here
the odd working building or flaking house punctuated the
half-farmed water meadows. Higher ground, further away,
became visible as a line of low hills closing towards the flat
river valley from my left. At the enamel sign, posted on metal
channel, with its back towards me, a grey Jaguar with
steering-wheel on the left for Continental driving was drawn
up on the grass verge. The road is very small, narrow, perched
along the river bank. No one uses it much.

I pulled in behind the Jaguar and clambered out to
stretch, stiffly, in the gathering sun. My bruised jaw still
ached. Working it a bit, I walked round the empty saloon
car and looked at the sign, which pointed up an earth path
beside a thick hedge. Rust streaked the chipped cream
enamel behind the dark blue letters that said '*Monument
Talbot. Guerre de Cent Ans*'. The small field beyond was
cordoned like a no-man's-land with wires and posts on
which vines grew two or three feet high. Two large hens,
Sussex Reds by the look of them, but probably a local brand,
were clucking and groaning irritably about. Across the field
an open farm shed with corrugated iron roofs housed ranks
of dried corn cobs and dilapidated agricultural equipment.

It was a mundane, smallholder's scene; everyday working land; hard to think of slaughter, despair, terror, an empire lost around here.

The path led down the side of the thick hedge, which was on my right. Some kind soul had planted roses along the left, to separate the edge of the gravel path from the vineyard. At the end, round the corner of the hedge, stood a tall stone pillar on a cracked base, supporting no Nelson at the top but a painted, rusted cast-iron Madonna, holding her child, arms outstretched, to the world. Under it, clad casually but elegantly in a light oatmeal jacket, lightweight trousers of a similar hue and a crisp shirt and tie stood Sir Richard White, looking first at his watch and then at me, with dry, neutral calm.

'Impeccable,' he said unenthusiastically. 'At least your timing is perfect. Good morning, Mr Simpson.'

'Good morning, Sir Richard.'

He held out his hand and we shook formally, Continental-fashion. My eye traced the inscription on a marble plaque at the bottom of the column, engraved in simple characters and hard to follow, except where dirt had emphasized the letters with its natural etching:

BATAILLE
de
CASTILLON
17 Juillet 1453
En ces lieux
Mourut le Général
J. Talbot

Cinqucentenaire 17 Juillet 1953
Municipalité de Lamothe

He let me look at it for a bit before speaking, letting the strangeness of the site of the rendezvous sink in. 'I was told,' he said eventually, 'that you have a strong, if not a powerful, sense of history. It seemed to me that this might be a very suitable place to meet.'

Behind me stood a much older-looking monument; a short, broken, cement-covered cross on a humped base. I looked at it curiously for a moment before looking back at the sliding grey river and quoting the lines that came unexpectedly to mind.

'"The plaintive numbers flow,"' I said, putting my hands into my pockets, '"for old, unhappy, far-off things; and battles, long ago."'

I said it half-jocularly to try and shake off the feeling of damp sadness that battle monuments give me, but the mists of morning had obviously imbued Sir Richard with a certain amount of melancholic reflection. His eyebrows raised themselves and his countenance opened to me with awakening nostalgia.

'Keats,' he said, as though doubting his ears. 'My favourite poet. I didn't know that you were a literary man.'

I didn't like to disappoint Sir Richard of all people but I was in no condition to bandy apposite metre from the Romantics with him at that hour of the morning.

'It's Wordsworth, actually. I remembered it from E. P. Thompson's book on William Morris. He used it to illustrate how the Romantic poets, including Keats, led that whole lot into the idealized Arthurian legend bit. Malory and all that cra—er, stuff.'

Sir Richard's eyebrows had come down again, sharply. 'E. P. Thompson?' he queried incredulously. 'You don't mean that—that—'

'Socialist historian, yes. And anti-nuclear campaigner. I'm afraid my attention wandered in the second half of the book because it deals with the history of the Socialist movement, but the first half is very good.'

A slight and condescending smile had taken over Sir Richard's face. 'Well, at least he left some memorable lines from a great poet in your mind, so he may have done some good after all. You know the history of this place, presumably?'

'Not really. It was the last battle of the Hundred Years' War, wasn't it? When the French finally chucked the English out?'

He nodded. 'It has great lessons for us, even nowadays. The English had won lots of battles—Agincourt, Crécy— using their famous archers and courage to muddle through. Their general, Old Talbot, was seventy-five years old; the terrifying sixth Earl of Shrewsbury and Waterford. He was a horrendous legend to the French for battle honours but he met his match here. Modern technology in the form of the cannon fire of a self-made technician called Jean Bureau. Talbot rushed a small force of his men against Bureau's cannon park, entrenched up against the Lidoire in a fortified camp over there—' he waved a hand across the vine-lined fields towards the low hills—'and they were massacred. Just one shot killed six men. They broke when a force of a thousand Bretons came down off those hills and took their flank. They ran for the river here to try and cross at the Pas de Rozan, where they thought they might get over. Old Talbot rallied a guard to cover them and was killed. So were most of the rest.'

I peered at the inscription again. 'So that was Le Général J. Talbot? Poor old bugger. Seventy-five? He must have seemed like Methuselah; the average lifespan was around thirty-five then, wasn't it? He was like a man of a hundred and fifty is to us now.'

Sir Richard nodded sagely. 'Indeed. He was wearing a purple bonnet and a crimson satin cloak, having promised the French during a four-year captivity that he would never wear armour against them again. So, devoid of his protection, he wasn't too difficult to kill. It was a terrible disaster. Took the English years to grasp that it was all over and they had lost the war.'

I squinted up at the Madonna twenty feet above us, proffering her child. 'I must say it seems pretty decent of the locals to have stuck up this monument, considering how the French feel about that war and the pillage that went on around here. Perhaps they see it from a different point of view, though; a victory, I mean. But why, then, commemorate Talbot's death and not, say, Bureau's victory?'

He shook his head gently. 'I'm not sure. I suppose that no one in England knows of Old Talbot now but the people of Castillon were on the English side, you see. The Hundred Years' War wasn't anything like most history books tell it. Round here, it is still vividly recalled. Indeed, up in my neck of the woods, much further inland, when they talk of the "war" they aren't talking about Hitler or the Kaiser; they're talking of the Hundred Years' War. So perhaps Talbot is still a powerful image to them, like Napoleon is to us. I prefer to think of this place in terms of the lesson we should all learn about old ways as against the new world. The French in modern times have taken to technology with enthusiasm, have outpaced us in so many fields, while we still cling to our traditions, our archers. The lesson from 1453 is still there for us.'

His voice had started to rise, to take on the rhythm of a man expounding a favourite theory, an evangelism. I had been about to disagree with him and I decided not to. In my recollection of the Hundred Years' War, twenty-five years after an enthusiastic exposition by a young school-master, it was all about a small, poverty-stricken nation called the English, who attacked, pirated and plundered a vast, powerful, wealthy country of twenty million called the French. It was really all about plunder but was sanctified by grandiose monarchic claims. Once the vast powerful nation managed to get its act together it seemed inevitable to me that the small violent one would get its come-uppance, and that is what happened. But we all have our different versions of history, most of them misleading, and it would not have been tactful to cross him.

'Change is inevitable,' intoned Sir Richard. 'It is a lesson we must all learn, a thing to embrace. I'm sure I don't have to lecture you, of all people, on this; indeed, it is why you are here today.'

'Sir Richard?'

'I agreed with Jeremy yesterday that it would be better if you were involved. I had not realized that in your—er— varied industrial career you were, at one time, involved in work for a tissue paper company?'

'Yes, Sir Richard. At one time I did have a client converting tissue. Some years ago.'

'Good. That experience will be very useful, I'm sure.' He looked at me and smiled his slight, distant smile. 'And I think that you may find a visit to a Grand Cru château of interest?'

'Grand Cru? Château?' I looked about me blankly. 'I suppose this area produces what they call Côtes du Castillon? I didn't think there was a château here?'

'Not here, of course not.' Sir Richard's voice was testy. 'I am not talking of this region. This was a convenient point to meet you on my way in from my house, up beyond Bergerac. We shall be going a few miles further that way, towards St Emilion. But before we go you had better tell me all about this other business.' His face took on a puckered, distasteful look as he stared at the dark bruise on my jaw. 'I am referring, of course, to the appalling violence you have once again attracted to yourself.'

CHAPTER 2

The letter arrived at my office in Park Lane on a bright morning in early June, when the trees across the road in the park opposite were in full leaf but still fresh, without that blown, tired look that they get in July. Although it was warm, the nine o'clock temperature was moderate and I felt energetic, ready for the dash to Euston and the train-ride up north that faced me that day. Being preoccupied and busy, gathering papers together, I gave the letter a fairly cursory reading. It was handwritten in a rather scratchy female script and gave an address in Meudon, which meant little to me. We get quite a few letters like that as a result of some of the promotional shows we do, in which people offer things to the Art Investment Fund, although very rarely from France. I flattered myself by reading it through quickly to show that my French was still up-to-date and stuck it in the pile connected with the Fund to be re-read and dealt with later. There were other, more pressing things to consider; Geoffrey Price, our accountant, was panicking about some missing cash-flow from our Chester office so Jeremy had asked me to nip up there to help deal with the problem. It meant dropping everything else for the time being and rushing to man the pumps. Cash-flow is a bit vital to an insurance broker's because you fund the whole business out of it—other people's cash, I mean—and there were some large numbers involved. The letter mentioned something about our commitment to British Art and I smiled at that as I got my briefcase loaded and put the Art Fund out of my mind. The Chester office and Sue Wester-man were much more important.

I had been peering at an involved computer print-out that made no sense at all when Geoffrey Price dropped his bombshell.

'I see that Sue's back at last,' he said cheerfully. 'You must be glad.'

'Eh?'

'Sue. From Australia. Wake up, Tim. Saw her last night at a party in Hampstead. Why weren't you—'

He stopped and caught my eye. 'Oh Lord. I am most dreadfully sorry. Didn't you—I mean, I thought that you and she—I—Christ, I'm sorry, it never occurred to me—'

I like Geoffrey Price. Always have. He's straight, sincere, hard-working and, for a married man, can still down a fair quantity of ale. In fact, for an accountant, he's almost human. So I didn't bash his skull in, as my first instincts dictated, and I didn't fire a string of obscenities at him, as my second ones did. I put down the stupid print-out and left the room, feeling that numb feeling that a really serious knock gives you, like a sort of concussion. The Chester débâcle faded into the distance.

I tried calling her at the Tate Gallery, where she must have been back at her job and I tried one or two of her old friends in Hampstead, which is where I originally met her, at a party of Geoffrey's, but there was no dice. Either I was unlucky or, more likely, she was avoiding me. I caught the train to Chester wondering whether she'd deliberately let herself into Geoffrey's orbit to get at me or what. While I was in Chester I put through some calls to the Tate but somehow she eluded me or the fates were against it—as flies to wanton boys, so are we to the Gods, or something like that—so it all added to the sense of anger and frustration that I was feeling for the week after the letter came in. In fact, if it hadn't been for the sudden, unexpected meeting at the Bank, I might have forgotten the letter altogether.

CHAPTER 3

'My uncle does think highly of you, you know,' said Jeremy White, breaking a long silence as the taxi turned into London Wall.

'I'm glad that I meet with Sir Richard's approval,' I answered shortly. 'There have been times, in the past, when I rather gathered he looked upon me as *non grata*, to put it mildly.'

Jeremy grinned. To our left, shielding the flaking modernity of the soulless buildings that fringe the Barbican, a broken section of pitted stone wall had been left, or perhaps deliberately constructed, to remind the passer-by that this had once been an ancient medieval city. It looked like a piece of bombed North Country factory that someone had forgotten to clear up. That's pure prejudice; I'm not fond of the City of London because I'm a West End man, myself. Park Lane, where I worked in Jeremy's bond-broking office, Knightsbridge, Piccadilly and Bond Street are my favourite stamping grounds or, at a pinch, Belgravia, but not the City. The City is a mean place, run by a bunch of gambling scrooges whose motto has always been, 'Never give a sucker an even break.' In the City you are either an arrogant waistcoated yahoo or you're one of the rest, on luncheon-voucher sandwiches and bread rolls. There's not very much room for the independent professional, like me, in the City. Oh, I know they've had to pay some quite decent salaries to the computer men and some accountants and lawyers, but only because they've been forced to by circumstances. A City man never gave anyone anything unless there was a pistol, real or economic, held at his head.

On top of my resentment towards the financial centre of Britain, I was feeling a bit liverish. Only twenty-four hours before I had been up north at the end of the first week of sorting out the difficulties at the Chester office. As one of Jeremy's closest aides and an ex-business consultant, I was frequently required to act as visiting fireman. Jeremy himself was unperturbed by things like cash-flow; he hired people like Geoffrey and me to keep his life peaceful. To Jeremy, life—working life, that is—was all about helping others to preserve money and to make more of it from their savings and investments. His bond-broking office and investment advice centre in Park Lane was officially an offshoot of his family's bank, White's Bank, in the City. In fact it had been Jeremy's own creation, quite independent and profitable, to the fury of his uncle, Sir Richard White and the rest of the family entrenched at the Bank, who regarded Jeremy as an upstart younger cousin who ought to be taught a lesson. Unfortunately for them, Jeremy was very successful.

To understand Jeremy was quite easy once you had grasped the fact that he had been brought up amid inherited wealth and property, which are constantly threatened by successive British governments no matter what their political hue or leaning. Just as a back-alley urchin, live as a cat, knows how to dodge the brickbats, the sticks and stones, the unsympathetic officers of law and education, and survive, so Jeremy, just as alert, knew how to duck and weave away from the probing taxman's lance. The aristocracy and the urchins have much in common in England; it is we stolid lot in the middle who make the sandwich filling between.

Jeremy's skill had formed the basis of a very successful business. Broking and bonding and advising had brought large sums of money to flow through our Park Lane office and a selection of branch offices poised among the affluent centres of Britain. Our cash-flow was over eighty million and a respectable brokerage clung to our fingers. Jeremy paid well, I thought; he had expensive tastes himself but he worked hard, enjoying it, loving the publicity and the drama of new insurance bonds, tax havens, dodges, loopholes, overseas placings, offshore funds, capital growth and interest rates. There was much more of the original merchant adventurer White, founder of the Bank, in Jeremy than in practically all the fusty, inert, ridiculously petrified family hangers-on at the Bank, fossilized in the City.

The taxi turned into Bishopsgate and, after a bit of swerving and wheeling, drew up outside the classical doorway of White's Bank, with its brightly-polished but discreet nameplates. The two huge doors were of Cuban mahogany, richly figured; an appropriate entrance for a bank founded on the fortunes of the original White whose adventures in the timber trade in South and Central America had

launched the family wealth. Jeremy paid off the taxi and a
flunkey in a footman-like uniform held the door, buttons
gleaming, as he bowed obsequiously to a recognizable member of the family. Jeremy winked at me.

As we walked into the foyer, past the huge doors, a
black-suited majordomo came out from behind a partition
and, seeing Jeremy, cringed respectfully. His gaze flicked
over to me, taking in the regulation pinstripe, the light blue
shirt, the black brogues and the battered Antler briefcase.
His features prepared to harden into a condescending grimace until, noticeably, he saw my tie. A look of grudging
respect, not too intense but respect nevertheless, crossed
his face. I should bloody well think so; that tie cost me fifteen stitches, a broken nose, two broken collar-bones and a
knee that acts up like hell every time the damp weather
turns cold or I have to drive for too long sitting in one
position.

'Sir Richard is expecting you, Mr Jeremy,' the majordomo
intoned. 'If you will allow me; this way, sir.'

Jeremy nodded absently and we followed the black suit
to a lift which, unlike any sensible lift, had to have an
incompetent old soldier in Corps of Commissionaires uniform to operate it. We ground up a single lofty floor which
I could have walked up in half the time and, after much
wrenching, clanking and blowing, the old lag got the cage
and outer doors open and stood, heaving and scraping
himself out on the carpeted landing, to allow Jeremy and
me to extricate ourselves. It occurred to me that for some
reason we were being given the full treatment; surely, under
normal circumstances, Jeremy would simply have strode up
the stairs and breezed into his uncle's anteroom with all his
usual aplomb. It was very suspicious.

Sir Richard's secretary was an attractive dark-haired lady
in her early thirties, smartly turned out in suitably subfusc
colours, who greeted Jeremy with a friendly smile and got
a charming beam in return. Indeed, Jeremy's tall, blond,

patrician figure positively made a leg at her in eighteenth-century fashion; Jeremy is as shrewd as anyone and knows full well where real influence often lies. He turned to me.

'Tim, may I introduce you to my uncle's secretary, Mary Waller? An absolutely indispensable lady who actually runs the Bank.' He burst into one of his high-pitched uncontrollable Etonian arpeggios of laughter. 'Tim Simpson, Mary Waller; Mary Waller, Tim Simpson.'

The lousy bugger hadn't clarified whether she was Mrs or Miss and I couldn't see the relevant finger—not that that necessarily means anything these days—so I just smiled and said how d'ye do like a proper gentleman. She was very pleasant.

'Hello, Mr Simpson. We have met before, just once actually, haven't we? That time you went to Brazil and popped in to see Sir Richard before you left. But I'm sure you won't remember.'

'Not at all,' I lied gallantly. 'I do remember, very well, although I'm afraid our encounter was brief.'

Her friendly smile turned into an even warmer one. She positively glowed at me. 'My goodness,' she said. 'How kind. And Trevor Howard has always been one of my favourites.'

'Bravo!' hollered Jeremy. 'You see, Tim? You've made a hit with Mary—very wise—can't go wrong here if Mary's on your side.'

She gave him a tolerant smile and, telling us that coffee would be coming along in a moment, ushered us into the presence. I was puzzled by Jeremy's remark; there was something afoot that I didn't like and I hadn't got much time to think about it because there we were, in the dark-panelled office of the Chairman of the Bank, with its portraits of past Whites looking down on us. There was an identical one of the Founder to the one that Jeremy also had over his own mantelpiece in Park Lane, showing the scallywag in a blue coat, silk breeches and stockings. Not a bad get-up for a timber trader who spent most of his life up the Amazon, buying mahogany and rosewood and doubtless siring half-caste children. At the end of this, the best office in the building, with its long windows overlooking the street outside, was a large pedestal desk, probably a genuine Georgian one, with some neat folders, a large blotter, as though anyone sensible still uses ink nowadays, a silver photograph frame and some other utterly conventional boring artefacts of business. Behind it, now standing up and coming towards us, was the spare figure of Sir Richard White, Chairman of White's Bank and currently the senior member of the family on a sort of Buggins's Turn basis.

'Good morning, Richard,' said Jeremy, in what I thought was perhaps a bit of a familiar form of address, knowing the acerbity of their past relationship as I did, but then who was I to judge family matters? 'I think you've met Tim Simpson once before?'

It must have been early two years since the events in Brazil which had caused a reluctant Sir Richard to use my services, borrowing me from Jeremy due to a shortage of suitable ferrets of his own at the Bank, and I could hardly remember his features clearly from the one rather gruff briefing that he'd given me at the time. I remembered him as being tall, slight, grey, rather wiry, perhaps in his early sixties and a bit dyspeptic. This morning, however, he seemed relatively affable and, as he came forward, a neatly-clad figure in charcoal grey pinstripe with waistcoat, he glanced briefly at my tie, as his minion had downstairs, then at his own and smiled thinly.

'Snap,' he said. 'How do you do, Mr Simpson? I remember you well. Mine was for rowing; I know what yours was for.'

His reference to our mutual Hawks Club ties, and the qualification for membership, which is a blue or a trial cap for Cambridge in one of a multiplicity of sports, was not the main cause of the sense of surprise I felt. I had always assumed that Sir Richard, like Jeremy, had gone from Eton to Oxford. Well, well, I thought, here's a promising start, anyway.

'How d'you do, sir?' I chimed. 'First and Third, I presume?'

He inclined his grey head in an affirmative bow. A lot of Eton oarsmen used to gravitate to Trinity College where, after various factional and private ventures on to the waters of the Cam, the remnants of the three rowing clubs that the college once boasted have been boiled down to First and Third Trinity Boat Club. Sir Richard waved us to chairs and Mary Waller brought in the coffee, which I needed badly. I had trained down the night before at Jeremy's urgent summons, relayed by his secretary Penny, slept fitfully in my neglected flat in the Fulham Road, and been waylaid as I entered the Park Lane office by Geoffrey Price, who needed some Chester statistics from me urgently. This left no time to talk to Jeremy before we were in the taxi and one of our legal experts begged a lift with us as far as St Paul's. I was, therefore, liverish and nettled. For the best part of three years I had tried to train Jeremy to prepare for meetings properly, but he preferred to fire from the hip and he was getting too old to change; I suppose that once a man's past forty you can't do much about him.

Sir Richard took a fastidious sip of his coffee. It was Wodehouse's Bertie Wooster who described rowing as a sport in which they put a piece of wood in the water, give it a shove, and take it out again. It's a misleading view, even if technically accurate as well as amusing, because rowing attracts all sorts. Just as we muddied rugger oafs turn out a high proportion of doctors, so the rowing world has its intellectuals and some rather donnish, ascetic types of men. Sir Richard was not exactly donnish, but there was an element of the academic in what seemed otherwise to be a traditional, bird-slaughtering, upper-rank Englishman. I waited deferentially for him to pipe up; Jeremy sat genially upright, blond hair gleaming in the dusty City light as he plied cup and saucer from lap to tray.

'I expect you're wondering what this is all about,' Sir Richard finally began, rather dolefully. I nodded brightly but he ignored my response. 'The fact is,' he went on, staring somewhere past my shoulder, 'that there are to be some changes here at the Bank. With immediate effect. Not one, but two members of the Board have decided to opt for early retirement and have relinquished their directorships.'

Good God, I thought, startled, there must have been a Night of the Long Knives. Members of the White family, once on the Board, were famous for hanging on to their places until the coffin lids were finally nailed down. To prise a member of the White family loose from his directorship was like getting a bull-terrier's jaws off a rat. This would mean some shifts in the political placings within the Bank and I wondered quickly what effect it would have, if any, on our own separate identity in Park Lane.

'I had hoped,' Sir Richard intoned rather mournfully, 'that the changes involved would be covered by senior executive directors from one or two of our overseas companies returning from abroad to take up places on the Board here. James, for instance, my second cousin in Brazil whom you've met, and my son-in-law Peter Lewis, who has recently been most successful in the Far East. However, they are in charge of independent autonomous companies and I'm afraid that such is the level of personal taxation in this country that both of them have absolutely refused to even consider returning here.'

Bloody sensible fellows. Besides, I thought, I can't for the life of me see what that old curmudgeon James White, who is as colonially Brazilian as the taste of good coffee, would have in common with life in England in the early 1980s. He'd certainly have more sense than to come over here; he'd loathe the place.

'So,' Sir Richard went on, regret seeping into his voice,

'I am happy to tell you that Jeremy, who as you know has set up and developed one of the Bank's most successful ventures of recent years, has agreed to join the Board of the Bank here as an executive director.'

I nearly, very nearly, dropped my coffee on to Sir Richard's best quality pale grey Wilton. For a moment I was utterly stunned. It wasn't just that the old buzzard had used phrases like 'most successful ventures' when all the world knew how bitterly he and his Board had tried to stop Jeremy, hamper his each and every move, ridicule him, hating his flamboyance, his flair, his taste for publicity; it was that they'd offered him anything at all. They could still surely have kept him off the Board? What the hell was going on? I stared at Jeremy, who smiled back blandly.

'Con-congratulations,' I croaked at him, almost choking on a forgotten mouthful of coffee and still not believing it. He inclined his head gracefully, the blond patrician head of a confident freebooter in his early forties.

'Thank you, Tim.'

'Yes.' Sir Richard's affirmation was neutral in tone. 'Well, as a result, Jeremy will be moving here to the Bank and although he will, of course, always take the responsibility for Park Lane and its operations and retain a seat on the board of that company, a new day-to-day chief executive will have to take over. Geoffrey Price, who I seem to recall was recruited by you when you were acting as a business consultant for us, has been offered and has accepted the position of managing director.'

A very sharp pang of disappointment shot through me. It wasn't that I didn't think that Geoffrey was competent, indeed he was, in a thorough, determined accountant sort of way, but it meant that the whole operation would lose Jeremy and I would be stuck in a rut, unsuitable for the top-line job. My feelings were very mixed. I wasn't sure if I felt rejected yet because Sir Richard didn't give me time.

'There have also been a number of, er, changes in management structure here which affect some of our executives. Jeremy has many times spoken with admiration of your professional qualities and I was, as I'm sure you know, very impressed with the quick audit you did for us in Brazil—' I didn't officially know because he'd never had the decency to tell me himself but still, better late than never I suppose— 'and it is therefore quite fit and proper that I, as Chairman of the Board, should offer you a position here with us as professional adviser. Your actual title would be Business Manager. We have several, of course.'

Another shock. More long knives must have been in action, indeed the Bank had now become the scene of wholesale slaughter and I almost glanced at the floor to look for bloodstains. Having made it quite clear that he had perforce to accept Jeremy on to his Board with ill grace, Sir Richard was now making as good a job as he could of offering me a post. I had to admit to myself that for a man doing the equivalent of swallowing strychnine, he was making a passable job of it.

'May I ask to whom I would report?'

He looked surprised. 'To Jeremy. As your immediate superior, that is, although I, of course, as Chairman of the Board—'

So that was it. I shot Jeremy a withering glance and he had the grace to look abashed. He was as sharp as anyone; he wasn't going to enter this nest of vipers, all laying in traps for him, without protection, and I was to be it. Shotgun guard, personal detective and dagger man to Jeremy until, at least, he was established here. Not for me the respectable headship at Park Lane, like dear old Geoffrey Price, the sound, married, offspringed conservative.

'I'm sure that your professional experience in consultancy and your ability in various foreign languages—that reminds me, weren't you at St George's, Buenos Aires for part of your schooling?'

'Briefly, Sir Richard, yes. Before returning to England.'

'I see. Well, that could be very useful in certain of our South American ventures.' He didn't elaborate for what purpose. 'Anyway, I'm sure it will be of great value, now that we are contemplating projects in—'

I was getting the picture. Not for me the settled life of a head of department even, with a reasonably predictable domestic life. It would be on planes and off them, all over the place—

'—so what do you say? Your salary will be for negotiation with your chief, who is of course Jeremy. I'm afraid I find it embarrassing to discuss such matters, but within the structure laid down by the Bank I'm sure that—'

Scrooges. Structure laid down by the Bank. I would bet good money that Jeremy would have to bend the rules to give me what I was earning now, on his generous scale at Park Lane. I managed to smile wanly. After all, what options were there to consider? If I stayed at Park Lane it would be to wither away in a backwater as Geoffrey's factotum. I could leave, but I hadn't given any thought just then to the question of what to do next. Of course if I had considered carefully before, I would have seen long ago that the logical progression in White's would be to the Bank itself but it had all happened quickly, unexpectedly. I might as well give it a whirl.

'I am very pleased to accept, Sir Richard,' I said, sealing my fate. 'And thank you.'

'Splendid. Splendid.' He put on a warm look. 'Welcome to the Bank. Now there is one other thing; it is you, is it not, who takes personal responsibility for our Art Investment Fund?'

I liked that touch. 'Our' Fund indeed. He had hated the thing from the start. 'Yes, Sir Richard, Jeremy and I had the idea originally, but I do—'

'Quite. We have decided that you should retain that responsibility—I believe that you enjoy it—and therefore its management will be moved with you here to the City.'

'I see. Thank you.'

'We do hope, therefore, that its future activities will not be attended by the rather lurid events which have accompanied its progress to date.'

Bloody cheek. I mean, I couldn't help it if there had been the odd dealer lost, like Willie Morton, Belgy Klooster or Peter Blackwell while I was in negotiation with them over some article or another. The Art Investment Fund was what you might call a longer-term investment fund for clients who wanted to get in on the art market without actually having to buy a Rembrandt themselves. We spread the money across a number of things in that field like paintings, silver, furniture and so on. It had been the original cause of my joining Jeremy and we had had some fun and games with it.

'—and apropos of the Fund, I have a request for you, a suggestion I would like from you.'

'Sir Richard?'

'We have a project, a very confidential project which I cannot describe to you now, in which we at the Bank propose to contribute a work of art, to be more precise a piece of sculpture, as part of a building in which it will be placed in the foyer. It does not have to be large but it would be appropriate if it were British. What do you think?'

'Well, Sir Richard, I'm sure that the Royal Academy would be glad to recommend several modern sculptors whose work you could examine and—'

He shook his head vigorously. 'No, no. It must be a work of an historically accepted master. The Fund would own it as an investment, so you see—'

My God, what a bunch of Scrooges. The generous Bank who would contribute a work of art with a fanfare of publicity would, in fact, keep it carefully as part of their own Investment Fund, quietly appreciating in value. There is no end to City mendacity.

'In that case, Sir Richard, what about a Henry Moore?'

He looked quite shocked.

'All those huge women with holes in? Most inappropriate. Can't stand 'em.'

'I see. Well if you're insisting on a British work, perhaps something by Jacob Epstein?'

His face went quite mottled. 'Appalling! That frightful tomb of Oscar Wilde in the Père Lachaise cemetery! With those genitals! Really! We are a respectable merchant bank.'

'Barbara Hepworth?'

'Absolutely out! Unintelligible nonsense. Bears no relation to anything you can see in real life.'

'Oh.'

Jeremy was keeping magnificent control of himself but his chair was physically shaking with suppressed merriment. His eye caught mine and steeled itself with the sort of control that a boy learns at prep school when someone sticks a pin into him during prayers. I had several bones to pick with Jeremy and I wasn't amused; Sir Richard's taste was obviously utterly traditional, hardly in any possible way avant-garde—

Then I thought of it. The French letter, oops, sorry, the letter from France. On my desk, still unattended to.

'Sir Richard, would you be prepared to consider a work by a foreign sculptor recognized as a superb master of the classic school but of a British subject? As an alternative?'

He looked guarded. 'Possibly. What have you in mind?'

'I have been offered—no, I have been advised from France—that there may be available a representation of the artist Gwen John, by Rodin.'

'Rodin? You mean the French sculptor who did that very suggestive couple called The Kiss?'

'Yes, Sir Richard. Rodin was very, er, concerned with female beauty but is regarded as one of the finest sculptors and his work is quite classical in many ways; indeed, his inspiration was from the Gothic.'

'Gwen John? Was she anything to do with Augustus?'

'His sister. A fine painter in her own right. Regarded by some people as a better painter than Augustus, if much less flamboyant.'

'Good grief. They were Welsh, weren't they?'

'From Tenby, Sir Richard, if you count Pembrokeshire as Welsh. Many people regard it as a sort of English—'

'It doesn't exist any more,' he practically snarled. 'Some bloody fool has called it Gwent or Clwyd or Gwynedd or Daffy or some other damn stupid name. But this bronze is in France, eh?'

'The letter came from an address in the Rue Babie, Meudon. A Madame Boiteau. But it didn't say a bronze, simply a work.'

'How much would it be worth?'

'I can't say. Bronzes by Rodin have fetched anything between fifty and a hundred thousand pounds at auction in the last year or so and this, if it is genuine, might have a great rarity value. Gwen John lived in utter poverty in France, modelling for a few coppers to eke out, and she had a great affair with Rodin. Like many other ladies. I only know of two works depicting Gwen John by Rodin. One is known as Whistler's Muse, in plaster, of which a bronze was issued much later, and the other is a marble bust. It would be quite a coup to find another.'

'Indeed! And most, most appropriate! I cannot tell you more, Mr Simpson, but you have had a rare flash of intuition. I wish you to pursue this matter with the utmost vigour. The utmost vigour. Keep me posted. Jeremy, I'll rely on you to keep behind this as well.'

'It will mean that I'll have to go to France, Sir Richard.'

'Of course you will. Of course.' He was suddenly quite excited. His thin frame tensed and his eyes glinted. After emphasizing his interest again and practically discounting my warning that the piece might not be a bronze or even genuine, he wound up the meeting by telling us of the arrangements for our arrival at the Bank, when announcements were to be made, and so forth. He even accompanied us to the door. As we reached it he said, with what seemed like an attempt at warmth, 'Once again, welcome to the Bank, Mr Simpson.'

'Thank you, Sir Richard.' I seemed to have been saying it all morning.

'I'm sure Jeremy will keep you busy. We are passing through a trying time, as I'm sure he'll tell you and someone with your, er, expertise, fieldcraft and tenacity will be a great asset.'

There didn't seem much I could say to that, so I just smiled the cheerful smile of Honest Tim, your pet bull-terrier and boy scout combined. Fieldcraft and tenacity indeed; what did he take me for?

'The practical work you did for us in Brazil was of great value,' he went on condescendingly. 'Our activities here are on rather a larger financial scale, of course, and it will obviously take a little time for you to pick up the threads, so to speak, but I'm sure Jeremy will guide you in the way in which we work.'

An American would have said operate. To be fair to Sir Richard, he probably sincerely believed that joining the Bank must be the ultimate ambition of anyone connected with White's in any part of its empire. It was an accolade reserved at senior level for members of the family, City gentlemen of excellent experience and pedigree, particularly ex-Guards officers and landed gentry, fox-hunters, stock-brokers and other bankers of the same ilk. I was not joining at senior level, of course, and in a sense I was immediately conscious of wasting my time. The way to the upper reaches of the Bank was almost certainly blocked to me so that the most likely progression in a career there would be by conveyance to one of the overseas subsidiaries in true colonial fashion. I was getting a bit old for that, I thought; there used to be a saying that you had to be a bright young man in the City when you were in your twenties, not your thirties. At my age I would be considered not so much the bright young man as the experienced old technician and I shot Jeremy another look but he just returned a bland anodyne smile.

'It'll be a bit of a scrum for you at first—' Sir Richard made another attempt at mock-heartiness— 'but I'm sure that's just your métier, eh? That last try against Oxford— I remember it well—tenacity—let me see—what year was it—'

Over ten years ago. And when I touched down their entire pack collapsed on top of me. It was the start of my bad knee, I thought, grimly. I was a fresh-faced keen young Simpson then, in my early twenties, with all the world before me and clear ideas of what was the right thing to do, not the man you see now. There is nothing in the world so passé as yesterday's sporting hero.

'—how on earth you did it. The entire pack seemed to be hanging on to you.'

Sir Richard was looking at me intently, like a fancier examining a prize pigeon. Somehow it wasn't a very flattering interest; there was a kind of zoological curiosity about it that excluded admiration.

'I'm flattered that you remember it,' I said shortly. 'I suppose that I really didn't think about it much. We were going to lose unless someone did something so I put my head down and went.'

He gave me the same intent attention for a moment more and then he nodded slowly. There was a silence. 'Admirable,' he said eventually. 'Admirable. Tenacity. Well, good day to you both.'

Jeremy and I avoided the wheezing lift and walked down the marble stairs in silence, which gave me the time I needed to frame a few choice sentences for him in my mind. The flunkey got us a taxi and, as we got in, I opened my mouth. Jeremy held up a magisterial hand to stop me.

'Not now, Tim! Not now! Not until we've celebrated at the works canteen while I explain. Cabbie! To the Mirabelle in Curzon Street.'

It wasn't until I settled back into the seat beside him and shot him another angry stare that I realized that I had just accepted a job in a district that I utterly despised. It just shows what age and a spirit of compromise can do to your principles.

CHAPTER 4

'I know, Tim, I know!' Jeremy refilled my glass, emptying the bottle of Dom Perignon. Near us, airing in its cradle, the Château Pavie 1970 waited for our attention; that was Jeremy's choice too. He and I argued from time to time, in futile fashion, about the merits of claret as against burgundy. I prefer to take my tannin in tea. 'You really are absolutely livid, I know. I owe you the most tremendous apology, really I do. You have it. Unreservedly. We have worked together supremely well up to now and I have been guilty of taking you for granted, disgracefully.'

'How many times have I told you,' I responded hotly, 'no surprises in meetings? Eh? And why the blazes couldn't you have warned me before we got there? In the taxi? And just to give it the full works, why couldn't we have met him tomorrow, after I'd finished the first phase at Chester? It would have been a sight more logical.'

His face took on a look of amazement and incomprehension. 'For Heaven's sake, Tim, haven't you got a diary? It's the Derby tomorrow.'

There's nothing a working man can reply to that so I let him go on, gently reproving me. 'I have apologized. Unreservedly. Your lobster bisque is going cold.'

'I'm sorry.' I started spooning the creamy soup down my

throat. 'But it was a real stumer, really it was. I was absolutely taken aback. There must have been the most incredible massacre down at the Bank. I'd better have some more bread to soak up all this lot. Did all this happen in the last week?'

'Yes. Well, more or less. That's when it came to a head, anyway. That's why I was so preoccupied. Distrait. That and—look here, Tim, this is really confidential and I've not told it to anyone, it's an absolute secret, but I owe it to you, it occupied my thoughts the whole way. I should have briefed you, but you see—well—the fact is that I'm going to get married.'

I dropped my spoon into the bisque and splashed my tie. I lose a lot of ties that way. Fortunately it is considered bad form to have a Hawks tie that looks shiny and new. Most of the chaps like their Hawks ties to look as though they've been worn for forty years by a dribbling geriatric uncle so I just dabbed vaguely at it with a napkin and tried to get a grip on things.

'You're going to WHAT?' I practically shouted, freezing a nearby waiter at a flambé tray and stopping conversation at the next table. Jeremy looked aggrieved. His tone was peevish. 'I say, now look here, Tim, there really is no need for that kind of reaction, damn it. Why shouldn't I get—' he lowered his voice— 'married, for goodness' sake? It's the right time. One is in one's early forties, you know. What on earth is wrong with you?'

'Jeremy,' I said faintly, 'I apologize for my outburst. You have, of course, my congratulations. But you—really—are you really, I mean—you'll change your lifestyle, will you, and settle down and all that? I mean, does the lucky lady know how you live right now, indeed, I'm sorry, I should have asked who is the lucky girl? Do I know her?'

He shook his head. 'I'm sorry. I can't tell you that, not now. Not that I can't trust you, I know I can, but you see I've promised, absolutely faithfully promised not to tell, so

I can't. You'd better have a glass of claret; you look quite shocked.'

I was. It had been a day, so far, to stand my life on its head. Park Lane was over, apart from the Art Fund; I was moving to the City, to White's Bank, to take part in unknown violence with financial yahoos; and now Jeremy, the arch-bachelor Jeremy, the business-fixated, nightclub gossip-column subject, the sailing, gambling, shooting Jeremy was going to find time for a wife. Don't get me wrong about him; there was nothing unnatural about Jeremy. Indeed, one weekend I'd spent with him sailing, taking Sue along, I'd been in no confusion as to what the relationship between him and the rather lush county girl he'd brought with him was, none at all. The noises against the bulkhead were entirely uninhibited. But marriage; that was another matter.

'It'll slow you down a bit,' I said. 'A wife. She'll want children, just at the time when you're joining the Bank. It'll be like riding a bicycle while perched on the crossbar. If you'll pardon the expression.'

He shook his head. 'It won't. I shan't. I'm not changing anything. She's agreed. We're staying in my London house, we're keeping the cottage and the boat will still be on the Hamble. She's got carte blanche to redecorate but I'm not moving and I'm not changing my work. Indeed, I—no, I'll modify that—we, Tim, you and me, are going to literally kick the stuffing clean out of that lot down at the Bank.'

His vehemence surprised me. Jeremy had always adopted a rather tolerant attitude towards the Bank, accepting both his independence from it and the respectable image it gave him without dwelling upon his subjection, as a junior mem-ber of the family, to the pressures and controls that the more powerful body imposed upon him. Now he seemed quite savage about it. I put a forkful of fillet steak in my mouth and waited for the next disclosure. It was clear that any contribution from my side was unnecessary; Jeremy was well wound up, now.

'Do you know what those idiots have done?' he demanded rhetorically. 'I'll tell you what they've done; they've lost three million this year. So far. And God knows what they'll really have lost by the time they produce their accounts, fudged though they'll be, for sure.'

I closed my eyes. There were times when Jeremy appeared to ignore entirely the full implication of what he was saying. In Park Lane we were set to make almost a million in net profit that year. Jeremy was telling me that I had just left a profitable, tightly-run, successful operation for a leaky, sick, hostile Bank in a location I would choose for the first missile target of World War Three.

'I know,' he went on, misinterpreting my expression, 'it's appalling, isn't it? But what a challenge, Tim! What a challenge! Unless something is done quickly the result is easily foreseen. The institutions—'

I nodded. I saw it all, now. I put my head in my hands. 'The institutions, Jeremy, which means your friends the insurance companies for whom you do so much business and who own a substantial number of the Bank's shares, have said that unless something is done they will have to take a hand. Like, say, getting one of their friends the big five banks, who are loaning White's money to fund the losses, to step in, squashing the current Board with their big feet in the process, pick up whatever banking and overseas operations they fancy and close the rest down, selling the site of the Bank for a multi-storey car park or an ice-cream parlour or something really profitable like a betting shop.'

He filled my glass again. 'Do you know, Tim, you really do have a grasp of a—a scenario, I believe they call it. You really do.'

'And who better to help avoid that scenario than their appropriately-related friend and success story, Mr Jeremy White, who, if given a seat on the Board in place of one of the moribund old fogeys who is there now, would galvanize the action and thus reassure his friends, who are none other than the insurance companies, who hold voting shares to the percentage of—'

'Thirty per cent.' He leant across and patted my hand. 'Absolutely superb. Not a cue missed. Scenario-sniffer extraordinary, you are. Not just Jeremy White, though; Jeremy White and his proven management team. Which starts with Tim Simpson.'

'Pug-ugly number one. What about Geoffrey?'

'Oh, come on, Tim, you malign yourself. You wouldn't have liked the job at Park Lane, would you? You'd have been bored in no time. The Bank is a much bigger, more exciting game. Geoffrey is an excellent fellow, excellent, but much too safe for this, much too conscious of his accountancy principles. And we've kept the Art Fund, just for fun. For us. Of course one can't go striding into the Bank like Cromwell throwing the whoremongers out of the Houses of Parliament, there is a certain style, a code to be observed in these things, feelings to consider.'

'Poor old Sir Richard.'

'Poor old Sir Richard be blowed!' Jeremy's voice was savage. 'He's a typical ex-oarsman.'

'Oh, come on, Jeremy, there are some quite—'

'Rowing, my dear Tim, consists of sitting in a boat, facing the wrong way round, working like hell to go in a direction you can't see while being shouted at by an idle little poof in a peaked cap at the other end. It's absolutely typical.'

Jeremy has never been much of a physical sportsman and he has all a yachtsman's contempt for river rowing craft. He downed the rest of his glass.

'The only thing that endears one to Uncle Richard is his Hundred Years' War business.'

'His what?'

'Didn't you know? His hobby is visiting the sites of the battles of the Hundred Years' War—pity it ever ended, can't stand Frogs—all over France. Spends weeks at it. He's got quite a nice house in the Dordogne, although the area's been ruined by the British now—five hundred years too late. Schoolmasters and liberal claret-drinkers all buying derelict hovels and doing them up.'

'So Sir Richard not only knows parts of France well, he also speaks the language?'

'Fluently. Anyway, look here, Tim, back to the Bank. It's a case of softly, softly catchee monkey.'

'Some monkey.'

'Oh, come on, that's not the old Tim Simpson who tore into Park Lane nearly three years ago and sorted out all that hideous mess. Nor the whizzkid who up-ended the Brazilian perfume disaster. You'll love this, I know you will. Besides, you'll be so much better off. Think of that.'

'Better off?'

'Oh my dear Tim, I completely forgot. Completely. Your salary will automatically go to thirty-five, with rather better perks. Is that all right?'

'Thirty-five? Thirty-five what?'

'Thirty-five thousand pounds a year. I'm afraid that the Bank's ridiculous salary structure won't allow me to pay you more than that but it is a rise of ten thousand a year, isn't it? I mean, there has to be some compensation for working in a dismal place like the City so they do themselves a bit better there. I say, do you think if we promise not to drink any port, because you're not supposed to on top of champagne, we could split another bottle of this really quite reasonable claret? It's frightfully good for you, you know; you're looking much better than you did this morning, really you are.'

CHAPTER 5

Gwen John's gentle eyes look out of her self-portrait at you with obstinate, almost defiant calm. The brown hair is parted centrally and swept back over the ears as though to a bun but, in fact, to longer soft folds down the back of the neck. From her high forehead the long nose leads the eye down to the small, weak, sloping chin, just like her younger brother's. He concealed his, eventually, with a beard. The mouth is firm, quite determined. She is wearing a startling red check dress, with a black collar secured by a cameo brooch, and a shawl is draped around her right arm, just above the elbow. It is a painting regarded as one of the finest British portraits of the twentieth century although it only just makes it; it was exhibited in 1900 at the New English Art Club. Her professor at the Slade, Frederick Brown, bought it then and somehow it has made its way to the Tate. Most people prefer it to the more saucy one in a brown blouse, now at the National Portrait Gallery, also painted in 1900 but in a different mood in which she looked down at you from the corner of her eyes, not directly, as though anticipating the years in France yet to come. I find it impossible to choose between them.

From where I was standing in the lower corridor in the far back basement of the Tate Gallery I could admire the red-checked self-portrait with the same joy that I always get every time I see it. Grumble as I may about the way that the Tate has to banish so many of the modern British paintings I love into an obscure back alley, I am usually glad of the peace and quiet down there. The atmosphere is muted, calm, suitable for what is perhaps a minor school of apparently restrained passions. Next to her self-portrait, Gwen John's painting of Dorelia, her brother Augustus's most famous mistress, portrayed that lady during a youthful hike through France with Gwen, ignoring me entirely. Next to Dorelia, a painting by Augustus himself depicted a thick rustic couple in a field, either struggling in a fight or trying to embrace, it was not clear which. It was odd to think that upstairs, not very far from the clear, self-contained portrait, Rodin's lovers embraced in a cool, eternal, marble Kiss, symbol of his erotic passion and inspiration, some of which spilled dramatically into this quiet Welsh lady's life. With regret, after a pause, I walked back through the hollow corridors, past Willie Orpen's hatted model Emily Scobel, seated under his Dutch convex mirror, up into the formal brown glaze of the eighteenth-century galleries and the spectacular colours of the big Turners. Perhaps one day they'll put Gwen John upstairs too, properly, where she belongs. I turned the corner into the circular marble hall, where the columned gallery above opens its arches under the great hemispherical dome, glass-paned, that tops the lot, way above the potted palms. Sue Westerman was standing there, to one side, where she had finally promised to be.

It is hard for me to describe Sue Westerman objectively because of past history, but superficially I suppose she gives out an aura of attractive competence rather than, say, sultry passion She is tallish, brown-haired, clear-skinned, uses horn-rimmed spectacles from time to time, wears quiet, slightly tweedy clothes and might be mistaken for a young lady librarian of Garden City intellectuality and cleanliness who could be expected to be entirely in control of herself and her life. Her figure is what they sometimes call willowy and the first impression is of slender, slightly suppressed femininity, to suit the sort of Oxford graduate and ex-Courtauld professional you would expect to find in a major public gallery. In America they have thousands of imitations of girls like Sue from Ivy League universities, carefully cultivating the tweed check skirt, the fine brown wool pullover and the self-conscious, vaguely feminist lifestyle, diction and conversation that are the sought image of so many educated American girls.

On closer inspection you would see that Sue has a generous mouth, humorous eyes and a much more interesting figure. She is a genuine, one-hundred-carat English creation, is Sue; for my money she is the best thing that can happen to anyone and, once committed, an enthusiastic, inventive and warm-hearted girl. It gave me a dreadful pang just to

see her. Her absence in Australia had been a major disaster
for me, a wound worse than bullets. To be put below a
career-enhancing year in Australia in her list of priorities
had hurt, badly, so I had not behaved well about it, or been
frightfully understanding or anything bloody silly like that.
Quite the opposite. It didn't help to think that the first time
I'd got to know her had been here, at the Tate, over lunch;
somehow I hadn't had the guts to invite her to lunch this
time, not knowing how things stood.

'Hello, Tim.' Her voice was pleasant, neutral; she smiled,
hesitantly.

'Oh, er, hello, Sue.'

What should I do? I wanted to kiss her but she stood
slightly back, not responding as she might, not moving
towards me but keeping away, her hands folded down in
front of her and her head up, like a schoolmistress surveying
a flock of children assigned to her as a new class at the
beginning of a school year; a flock to be kept at arm's length,
disciplined. It both checked and irritated me. Damn it, I
thought, I'm not having this. Smiling cheerfully but as
neutral as she was, I stepped forward, as an old friend
might, took her shoulders in my hands and planted a kiss
on her cheek; not too chaste, you understand, not a peck,
warmer than that, the kiss of an old friend, someone familiar.
All right then: a past lover.

It was not what she wanted at all. She flinched backwards
and then stopped, tense, waiting to see what I might do, to
see if I might go further, perhaps impose in some way or
another, but I stepped back, as cleanly as a Frenchman at
a medal ceremony, and smiled at her. Her eyes, looking
deep into mine, showed relief. Well, well, I thought, it's
back to square one, Tim lad, no familiarity or rights due
from previous you-know-what, she's in a defensive, down-
Fido sort of mood.

'How are you?'

'Fine, thank you. And you?'

You wouldn't think, would you, that before she'd gone to Australia nearly a year or more ago, we had lived together for six months, laughed, loved, professed an undying devotion, the lot? That right bang shoot in the middle of it she'd simply up and accepted the Tate's offer of a year's transfer to a New South Wales gallery, leaving me alone like a shag on a rock? There's a fine sense of priorities for you: career first, Tim last; I mean, bugger you, boy, I'm off, don't forget to take your boots off before you go to bed, alone. No, I hadn't taken it well. The few weeks before she left had been pretty grim. I drank a lot and finally took her to the airport in silence. Apart from odd cards and two or three graphic telephone calls concerning a Godwin sideboard that I needed to know about, that was it. I supposed that she had been glad to be rid of me by the time she left. Nagging in my mind had always been the worry of finding out about her return and I wondered now, with grim humour, whether her meeting with Geoffrey had been an indirect notice or purely by chance.

There were some circular alcoves at the side of the marble hall, with white-topped round tables and black plastic-covered semi-circular benches curving inside them. I gesticulated at the nearest.

'Shall we sit down?'

'All right. I—I can't stay long, you know.'

'You said that once before.'

In the centre of the marble hall there is a large glass case with black edging containing a cool, naked, translucent marble female with a slender young figure, kneeling. She is holding a small ornamented box, almost sarcophagus-shaped, with mouldings, in her hands as she kneels. I realized, with a shock of recognition, that it was Harry Bates's depiction of Pandora, about to let loose the winds. A fat lot of good the big glass case would be if the marble lady got the box open.

'How are things at Park Lane?' Sue looked at me directly.

Bizarre, wasn't it? She was behaving just as a man might with a to-be-discarded lover, keeping it cool, neutral, unemotional. In normal circumstances, if there are such things, the woman is the temperamental one, hostile, defensive, or whatever she believes the situation calls for. My hackles started to rise; I hate being taught lessons.

'I'm leaving Park Lane,' I said shortly.

She glanced up sharply, curious, her face showing an emotion—interest—for the first time.

'I'm going to the Bank. Hasn't Geoffrey told you? He's going to be the MD of the Park Lane company. It's a step up for him.'

Mentioning Geoffrey was a ploy to let her know that I was in the picture. I was still boiling about his prior knowledge of her arrival home.

She shook her head. 'No, I didn't know. I thought you hated the City.'

'I do.'

'Then why?'

'Money.'

She shook her head again. 'I don't really believe that. It'll have something to do with Jeremy. What's happened? Are you leaving the Art Fund?'

'No, I'm taking it with me.'

'Oh.'

Oh, I thought, bloody oh, that's just about the size of it. Her interest in me comes down to the Art Fund and oh. I looked across the hall, sparsely peopled with strolling visitors in summer clothes, and got a grip on my question.

'Sue, why didn't you tell me you were coming back? I've spent a year trying to understand why you went and just about succeeding. Now I'm totally flummoxed.'

'Have you? Are you? That's not what I've heard.' Her eyes were accusing me of countless affairs.

'What have you heard?'

She shook her head, waving the soft brown hair yet again.

'It doesn't matter. I thought that after what happened before I left, you know what I mean, it was best to—I wanted to be free to decide on my own, to establish my life again.'

'Not as before.'

'No. Of course not, Tim. You surely didn't think that after a whole year I would simply walk back in, now did you? Especially after the way you behaved. I assumed it was all over, well, it was all over, wasn't it, you didn't write and—'

'I didn't write? You mean you didn't write, don't you, like you promised to?'

She bit her lip. 'Look, Tim, there's no point in going over all that, there really isn't.' Her voice was soft, troubled. 'I agreed to meet you because apart from what you asked for, well, you and I have to clear up the situation. I felt I owed it to you to let you know—well, things are different, aren't they, but I've been frightened to see you because, well, you must understand, surely?'

'Understand? No, I don't understand. You haven't explained at all. Or am I supposed to be frightfully decent and British about something I don't understand?'

'Oh, come on, Tim, it's been a whole year!'

'Whose bloody fault is that?'

'Don't shout! I'll leave now if you shout!'

'I'm not shouting. I'm sorry, but I'm not shouting. To find out from Geoffrey, that was unspeakable. At least you could have—'

'I didn't know how to tell you.'

'It can't have been that difficult, surely, I'm not a bloody homicidal maniac, am I, just to tell me—'

'That I'm engaged?'

I didn't hear that right. I sat looking at her blankly for seconds.

'You what?'

She licked her lips nervously and pressed them together.

Her eyes flickered away from mine. 'I'm engaged, Tim. To Arthur. We got—'

'Who the bloody hell is Arthur?'

She got to her feet. 'I'm going! You're shouting! I'm not—'

I grabbed her arm and jerked her down, back on to the black plastic seat. One or two heads that had swung round quickly swung back again as I glared at them like an anti-aircraft searchlight. She spoke in a low, intense voice as I let go the arm.

'Arthur was in Australia on an exchange too. He's a nice quiet gentle man in the museum service as well. Archæology. He'll be back soon and—'

The world seemed distant, hollow, cavernous, unreal, kicked in the head. 'My God?! All this time I've been half sick about you and why you wouldn't write you've been at it with some randy little Mortimer Wheeler, like—'

'How dare you!' She hissed with rage. 'How dare you drag everything down to your own despicable level! Arthur is charming, attentive, a gentleman. There has never been any question—no, I'm not going to—I refuse to drop to your—'

I gaped at her in disbelief. 'You've invented this! It's not real. Look, if you just want to get rid of me, you don't have to invent a ridiculous fiancé, you know.'

She flushed. 'I haven't invented him, you arrogant bastard! I've just told you: Arthur will be back soon. I met him four months ago, in Melbourne.'

'And you're engaged? You? Just like that? And you've never—you say he hasn't—' I sat back, still in a state of shock. 'I don't understand this. Either you're lying or he must be an absolute wimp.'

Her jaw opened. Her face was white. 'My God, you're incredible! Dreadful! Your attitude is typical! You haven't changed a bit, have you? You have no concept of relationships at all! Just because you think that a woman is something you come back to after a beer-soaked evening to strip off and lie down on, you think that—everyone is like—like you—where are you going?'

Her voice trailed away. I hadn't been conscious of getting up. It was as though the impact of what she said, the sheer rotten falsity of it, had lifted me out of my seat like a powerful ramrod. If ever I had really cared tenderly for a girlfriend it was for Sue; if ever I had behaved with gallantry until that fatal announcement of her intended departure to Australia, it was during our months together. I tried to move sharply back from her, as one confronted by a shocking apparition, but the bench was behind my knees and the alcove wall at my back. Somehow I regained my balance. Her eyes widened as I leant over the stricken white plastic table, pain and fury getting the better of me, to say the last words I was going to say, not shouting; hardly audible, they were.

'If that's the way you remember me and the way I behaved towards you, then you'll be glad to see me go, won't you? You and bloody Jeremy and Sir Richard and everyone else; you've got me down, haven't you, as the old oaf Tim, just a necessary attendant dog to be used and manipulated and escorted when it bloody well suits you and when you bloody well want it. A thick ex-rugger heavy with no sense or finesse at all. Well, good bloody bye, Sue Westerman.'

I had to worm my way out sideways from the bench in ridiculous, undignified fashion instead of being able to march straight away and she fluttered a hand at me over the white plastic of the table top. 'Wait, Tim, I—I had these notes, you asked something about Rodin and Gwen John—I've got—'

'Bugger Rodin. Stuff Gwen John. I'll find out for myself. No, I may not even bother.'

I ploughed out through the revolving doors past a quick-footed flunkey into the sunlight and down the stone steps that some stupid hippies were sitting on so fast that I trod on the hand of one of them. Serve him damn well right for sitting ostentatiously in the way. He shouted angrily, turned at me and then backed off quickly as I marched on. I was so mad and wounded that I turned left, ignoring the sight of the tug-barged river, and was past Millbank Tower before I began to take stock of where I was going. It wasn't until my legs started to slow and I saw the Houses of Parliament coming up that I veered off into some shady riverside gardens to try and calm down. My breathing eased. My sight cleared and I found I was practically nose-to-nose with a sculpture of six large dreary bronze blokes in rags. One of them was carrying a huge key.

'Good God,' I said, startled, 'that's the Burghers of Calais.'

Which is, as everyone knows, Rodin's version of an incident in the Hundred Years' War. It's strange how certain themes, once started, seem to pervade life for a bit.

CHAPTER 6

It's an odd thing, but getting so livid that day and walking out on Sue was probably the best thing I ever did, which all goes to prove what a mad game life is. There are times when the wisest thing you can do is to stop talking and clear off. Reflection and subsequent advice have made that clear to me now.

You have to go back to work in the end and, during the move out of Park Lane across to the City, I had time to brood on events for a while. I wrote back to Meudon to fix up a meeting; I packed up my files and catalogues, auction records and reference books. I read Susan Chitty's life of Gwen John and I re-read Michael Holroyd's of Augustus. I learnt the significance of the Rue Babie address. I bought several books on Rodin and I found an old one, in a second-hand bookshop, by Victor Fritsch, one of Rodin's assistants and a sculptor in his own right, like Bourdelle. It was some story. The people who write about Rodin, mostly Frenchmen of course, hardly even give Whistler's Muse a mention, let alone Gwen John. There are so many other famous works, famous mistresses, grand encounters, struggles for existence and for recognition with the established academies to bother with a small, slight affair with an obscure 'English' artist. She was only one of the dozens that Rodin bestowed his favours upon, late in his life—he was sixty-three when she modelled for him—and she hardly rates a mention when there are others like Camille Claudel and the Duchesse de Choiseul to dwell upon. Sculpture had never been one of my fortes; like Jeremy, I was comfortable with paintings, furniture, silver, porcelain, predictable domestic artefacts. Sculpture is different; I had to get the hang of the market; I was going to need help.

They allocated me an office on the third floor of the Bank, at the back, down a panelled passage. It didn't look out on to any trees, let alone a park. The view from the window was of more windows across a widish shaft between buildings and lots of brick. Fortunately the window had a Venetian blind on it so that I could imagine the dusty false horizontal striping falling on a Sickert or a Bernard Dunstan nude, voluptuous in my spare visitor's chair of upright teak. Mary Waller appeared one day with the old lag from the lift, grunting under the weight of a rubber plant which she had liberated from another office.

'There you are,' she said triumphantly, 'it looks so joyless in here. I'm sure you must be missing Park Lane.'

'Um, thanks,' I said, as the old lag rolled his eyes at me and left. 'I thought that the decor was meant to keep the mind concentrated on the making of money.'

As an antidote to the environment I had hung up a portrait of George Melly by John Bratby and she giggled as her eye took in the thick oil impasto of white, red, blue and green that assembled the flamboyant physiognomy.

'I don't think that's the sort of portrait that normally hangs in the Bank,' she said, delighted.

'This,' I replied pompously, 'is now the office of the Art Investment Fund. Let everyone remember that.'

Jeremy occupied a room just down the passage that was suitably impressive. It had belonged to one of the late unlamented family directors. Jeremy positively bloomed. It had long been his ambition to achieve recognition, to get inside, despite his outward scorn for the family headquarters which had managed for so long to repel this piratical boarder. He started to poke his nose into all sorts of affairs; files landed on my desk with irregular but constant frequency, so that I was kept busy. Other people at the Bank, once introduced, were not particularly warm except for the occasional business school graduate of suitable social background taken on by the Bank for obscure duties. It was a new world to get the hang of, unrelated to the personal financial services we had specialized in at Park Lane. The majordomo in the foyer managed to nod at me when I arrived every day, so recognition as an employee was imminent; I avoided the wheezing lift and its wheezing pensionable operator and walked up the three flights of stairs, partly as a keep-fit exercise and partly because the lift and its incumbent old lag irritated me beyond endurance. Patience has never been one of my virtues.

I went to an estate agent in the Old Brompton Road and got a sheaf of details of flats nearer to South Kensington Station. Somehow the break with Sue at the Tate finished off the tatty old place in the Fulham Road for me entirely. I could afford better now; memories in the old place were too intense, and not just of Sue; it was time to go. I reckoned that I could still stay in Brompton, one of my favourite haunts, and get the tube to Monument every day. From there it was a short walk up Gracechurch Street to the Bank.

Sadly, it did not compare with my No. 30 bus ride up the Old Brompton Road to Knightsbridge and Park Lane but it was idle to repine. I said to myself: Life's like that, Tim, the universe is expanding, change is inevitable. Who said that?

It was about ten days after our first meeting at the Bank that I rolled grumpily out of bed, drove down to Gatwick and caught the flight to Paris. The good thing about flying British Caledonian to Roissy is that they have the decency to serve you with breakfast, unlike many of the omnibus-planes from Heathrow, and so I sat back, after they took the tray away, and re-read the letter in omeletted satisfaction while we tilted down on our last few thousand feet to earth.

'Messieurs,' the scratchy hand began, 'I have had the occasion to note that your ancient and esteemed establishment—' the plane bumped on an invisible lump, up in the air, and the writing shot up and down as my hand jerked at that description—'has a reputation for good judgement in investment in works of particular significance in the history of English Art—' well, that was flattery for sure, but Jeremy and I had pulled off one or two agreeable coups even if we had never managed, in the end, to get a Godwin sideboard. 'I have, therefore, decided to write to you on the subject of a work—' yes, definitely the word was *œuvre*, not marble or bronze—'by the great Auguste Rodin himself, depicting the English artist Gwen John—' the French often lump us all under the description Anglais, failing to distinguish English from Welsh—'both of whom were, as you may know, illustrious residents here in Meudon for some time.' That was a real piece of Gallic euphemism, for sure. Rodin may have been an 'illustrious resident' but little Gwen John, obscure and self-effacing, could hardly be described in those terms.

My thoughts were interrupted by a whistling and crackling as the loudspeaker system announced our imminent arrival and demanded the fastening of seat-belts, the stub-

bing-out of cigarettes, folding of trays, uprighting of ver-
tebræ, clearing out of possessions when leaving, promotional
consideration of commercially-linked hotels, ground transport, onward flights, non-EEC forms and many other admin-
istrative half-advertisements, all subsequently repeated in
French. The pitch of engines changed, wheels clacked down,
mechanisms whirred, flaps flapped; the tartaned crew
jostled with the remaining breakfast rubbish. I put the letter
away resignedly. It had not been difficult while waiting for
Madame Boiteau, as she signed herself, to reply to my letter
suggesting that I call on her, to imagine some dreadful
spoof, a great practical joke, by an idiotic acquaintance or
media ham-artist, making the Art Fund, the Bank and me
look like ridiculous pomposities of greedy disposition. But
despite the lack of telephone number and the antiquated
form of communication a tenuous link had been established,
in its own way perhaps confirmed more strenuously, to bind
our interest and this old-fashioned lady together. Sir Richard
had been most emphatic; don't mess about, he had said,
waiting for photos, evidence, documents. Get over there, fix
a meeting, talk, otherwise a competitor will get in ahead of
you. I obliged, was obliging, queuing up at immigration
desks, however briefly, catching buses, lavishing lumps of
my precious life's time on errands of this nature. Fieldcraft
and tenacity, you might say.

The problem with going over to France or any other
Continental destination nowadays on business is the time
difference. You catch the earliest morning flight, which is
no longer at seven but at eight; you land at nine but it's ten
local time. You clear Customs and immigration, even if you
have no luggage, thirty-odd minutes later catch a bus or a
train to the centre of the city and find that it's eleven or half
past. You've lost half a day in return for getting up at six.
I checked into an hotel near the Etoile, washed and had a
light lunch. There was plenty of time to go out to Meudon
and I had no intention of rushing back. After the Boiteau

lady I might need to check on things, visit a specialist, talk to people. I finished the meal, strolled down the Avenue Wagram, looking at my watch; parsimony got the better of me. I decided to take a train instead of indulging in a taxi.

I got out at Meudon-Val-Fleury on the harsh electrified line and came out of the station to look at the grey buildings, the cement-edged stonework next to the steep-channelled tracks. It couldn't be far to walk. I bought a street guide at a nearby *tabac,* got my bearings and wove my way through to the Place Rabelais. The long, tree-lined Avenue Jacque-minot, named after the general who once owned the place, stretched up the hill in front of me and I strode briskly up it, enjoying the sunlight on the leaves and the flint-studded suburban villas on either side with their brick dressings. This part of Meudon is still a residential area, a bit congested with unplanned housing and gardens for a clear impression to be gained, sloping hard on the side of a hill. No shopping terraces or café-centre met my eyes, only the straight stretch of leg-bending avenue going directly up to the forest around the château at the top, beyond the Rue Terre Neuve. The Rue Babie came up quite suddenly on my left.

It was when I turned into the short street with its iron-railed fences and short front gardens on one side that the atmosphere came over me. It is almost sandwiched on the side of the steep hill it runs levelly along, the Rue Babie, its houses jammed briefly into the space available. No. 6 is a small, narrow villa of the French sort, with concrete-garnished railings and high, thin front door and windows edged in white paint. Brick inlay decorates the dun cement of the façade. Next to it, at No. 8, the garden stood deserted and overgrown.

For a brief second I couldn't believe it. The spare lot at No. 8 Rue Babie was bought by Gwen John in the nineteen-thirties. On the tangled neglected land had stood a wooden shack-cum-garage, unheated and tumbledown, draughty and insanitary, which she first used as a studio and then as a dwelling, to the horror of her brother and friends. She bought it with the proceeds of the sale of her paintings at the Chenil Galleries, the only time in her life when any capital came to her. Before she moved in she lived in the Rue Terre Neuve around the corner, in the attic of a house since demolished for a road-widening scheme. Like many artists, she ran the two establishments concurrently for a while before finally moving to the Rue Babie as a permanent abode. They have since knocked down the shack and built a modern, square cement villa on the site. It was deserted now, unused. The post, delivered assiduously into a void through the slot in the gate, lay in a wet pile of jumbled, sodden envelopes inside the entrance. The garden was weed-high, brambled, spiked with chestnut saplings. Tall poplars, limes and plane trees meshed in unpruned disorder around the fenced edges of the plot. Long grass and bushes waited for a caring gardener who had never come. At any moment I expected the modest, neat figure of Gwen John herself to come picking her careful way around the side of the villa towards me. She might never have left the place. For several moments I stood, staring through the railings, mesmerized. Somewhere on this plot, before the cement villa was built, stood the wooden shack she lived in, her canvases rotting, her cats prowling, the hundreds of sketches piled carelessly away. Around me the dull prosperous suburb of Meudon in modern times stood indifferent; no plaque marked the spot, no caretaker took the entrance fee of any gawping crowd. It was mundane, matter-of-fact, forgotten. The wretched poverty she chose to ignore, her religious mania, the final hallucinations and self-neglect, the hermitic, eccentric solitude for a moment infected me, taking my mind off my mission as I marvelled at the thoughts.

With a jerk I looked at my watch; I was almost late. The house of the Boiteau lady was just nearby, along the road. I could see it, a flint-walled half-terrace house with white shutters to the upper windows. Brick pillars stood on either side of an iron front gate and the iron railings of the front fence were set in a low concrete wall like others in the street. Walking to the gate, I swung it open, crossed to the front door with its wrought-iron panel and rang the bell.

There was no answer. The street was empty, deserted. At the far end an Algerian workman was sweeping the pavement. It was very quiet. I rang again, composing my features into an ingratiating grimace of pleasantry, rehearsing my opening phrases in French, smoothing my jacket, straightening my tie. Still no answer. This is it, I thought, dealing with private people instead of the trade or auctioneers, unreliable, you can't trust them; I bet it's a souvenir copy or a cheap plaster imitation, you never can rely on the judgement of the general population, I've wasted my time. Silly old Sir Richard.

The door opened. It was a shock. Instead of an old lady, or even a middle-aged one, a man stood behind it, using it almost as a shield, his face and figure half-concealed because he had only opened it about nine inches. Dark crisp hair covered a hard, powerful head. The eyebrows formed a black, straight line above dark brown eyes. A powerful jaw, set in a thick neck, emphasized the muscular strength of the body, big and tall, taller than me. The hand that gripped the door-jamb was no intellectual's; it was a working hand, knuckled, black-haired, a crusher.

'*Oui?*' The head jerked with the question in a typical Gallic gesture. Unpleasant, but I decided to be as polite as possible.

'Madame Boiteau?'

He shook his head. 'She's not in. She is not available, monsieur.'

I was nonplussed. 'Not in? But I have an appointment. Are you sure?'

'No. You are mistaken. She is not in.'

'When will she be back?'

He shrugged, a contemptuous shrug. His eyes flicked up and down me with the arrogant disregard of a Frenchman who cannot give a stuff for any foreigners, particularly English foreigners. I took a violent dislike to him. I've never been of Jeremy's persuasion about the French. Indeed, I'm quite the opposite, having spent too many nights after rugger matches, on tour in France, enjoying the hospitality of a friendly, civilized crowd of first-class rugger men to go in for that sort of attitude. On the whole I like them all, despite past history, but this was a nasty bit of work. I tried to fix him with a stare.

'There must be some mistake. Madame Boiteau wrote that today would be suitable.'

'No. You must have the wrong day. She has gone away. She will not be back until next week.'

This was impossible. I could see the faces of Jeremy and Sir Richard when I got back to tell them. 'You're absolutely sure? She left no message?'

'No.'

Helpful bastard, I thought. Really helpful. He stood there, defensive, door still only nine inches open, tense, waiting. I could have sworn that his nerves were bad.

'Please would you tell her that Mr Simpson called?' I felt foolish, incompetent, idiotic.

He jerked his head again. 'Who?'

I pursed my lips. It had been almost a deliberate insult. 'Mr Simpson of White's Bank. Here is my card.' I wrote the name of my hotel on it. 'If she should return will you please see that she gets this. Ask her to contact me. Before tomorrow.'

'She won't. I've told you; she won't be back until next week.'

'Look here—' I stopped. There was no point. He had at least taken the card. I stared at him, trying to make out what on earth had happened. 'I've come from London. She definitely wrote that today was all right. May I come in?'

He shook his head. 'You are mistaken, monsieur. It must be another date. She is not here. She is visiting her family, in the country.' He closed the door, finally, rudely, with abrupt decision; almost a slam.

'God damn it,' I said out loud. 'What a cock-up. Bloody hell.'

Too late, I put my hand into my pocket and pulled out the letter confirming the meeting. It was no use now. Anger seethed through me. There was something totally wrong. Could the old lady have had second thoughts and be sitting inside like Gwen John, refusing to see the American patron, Quinn? No; he was really strange, hostile. You know what the French are normally like; a mistake like that and they crowd round you, read the letter fourteen times, chatter, gesticulate, sympathize, talk about the old lady, run to the nearest *tabac* for news, suggest impossible alternatives. Not him. I turned slowly away and walked out through the iron gate, closing it after me.

At the junction of the Rue Babie with the Rue Général Gauraud nearby, I stopped to ponder. Further down, on the right, was the house where the philosopher, Jacques Maritain, had lived with his wife and her sister, Vera Oumancoff. It was to Vera that Gwen John brought a drawing or a painting once a week, having a crush on her in the strange way that she did on various women during her life. It was a street of strange memories, unremarkable now, inconsequential.

What on earth had gone wrong? I felt great sympathy for Quinn at that moment. At least Quinn had been visiting France anyway; I was here specially, damn it, it had cost money—

The girl who came down the road was dark and plumpish, pretty, wearing a cotton dress and carrying a leather hand-bag, an expensive one, slung on her shoulder by a strap. There was something about her that would make men glance at her again, speculatively, although she walked straight along the pavement looking ahead without a glance to right or left. Her high heels clicked sharply on the stones, firmly, and she seemed to be so purposeful that it was a surprise when the clip-clop of her shoes stopped. I looked up to see what had happened and saw to my surprise that she was outside the Boiteau house and was fitting a key into the lock.

What happened then was odd. Distinctly odd. As the door opened it moved suddenly, to open even wider; she went through the gap quickly, practically stumbling on the step. At the same time a tabby cat shot out beside her feet and streaked down the pavement followed by another, a striped marmalade cat which just got through the door as it slammed shut. The marmalade cat lit off down the pavement after the other one as though all hell was after it. The girl vanished, plunging into the house in a sort of lunge, as though drawn from within by a powerful hand. The closed door smacked to impassively, its faded wood slightly streaked by the weather. On either side, the long windows of the downstairs front rooms glinted in the sunlight. One of them was slightly open and suddenly, with a piercing scream, another cat, a black one this time, came spitting out through the gap, hair spiking as though electrically charged. It shot across the road under the wheels of a parked van as the window slammed shut. I gaped at the scene. Those cats were terrified. Absolutely bloody terrified. There was no doubt of it. I sauntered down the road back towards the house. Nothing made sense. Madame Boiteau had definitely agreed to meet me. I had the right day, the right time. Arriving at the front door again I stood hesitant, wondering whether to ring the bell again.

From within the house came the sound of a scream. An unmistakable scream, female, not feline, as of a woman in terror. Then a bang and a scuffling noise.

That did it.

The side of the house had a passage down it, along the

flint-embedded wall, and I scudded down it at a fast clip, hopping round the corner on one leg. At the back there were dustbins, a small yard, an outhouse and a kitchen door. I went through the kitchen door, which was unlocked, into a dark, tiled kitchen, through that and into the hallway beyond. On my right was a back room, door open, and through it I saw, vividly, a frail old woman tied to a chair, her head lolling back. One glance at the dropped eyelid, the frozen side of the face, told me that she was in the throes of a very bad stroke indeed.

At the bottom of the stairs a miserable scruffy-looking sort of bloke had hold of the girl, arms pinned behind her back, one hand clamped over her mouth. The powerful-looking man who had answered the door had hold of her from the front, lifting her as though to help carry her upstairs, none too gently. Her handbag was on the floor, burst open, and her cotton dress had ripped down the front, revealing a white bra. My first impression was that they were going to rape her.

'Oy!' I shouted.

The scruffy one had only just got time to jerk his head round, over his shoulder, to see me before I hit him a hard chop on the back of the neck, propelling him and the girl forward into the thickset man. He stumbled in turn and let go of the girl as they staggered, entangled, across the hall. The scruffy man fell over, either tripping on the girl's legs or groggy from the blow.

The girl, released, screamed loudly but it didn't stop the burly man coming straight for me. I struck at his neck as I sidestepped, getting a pretty solid hit where the neck joins the shoulder but he brushed it aside and hit me, right in the solar plexus, so fast that I had no time to block the blow. Silver spots danced before my eyes. I hit him back, once over the heart and another, a left I got in past his upraised arm, cracking hard on to his jaw and making his head jerk. Then he hit me back.

As I went backwards, slamming against the wall, I realized that I was in trouble. This bugger was no ordinary pug-ugly; he was a trained Parisian pro, lethal, a genuine gangster of the first mark, hard and solid, like a shark. Only a lucky crack with a metal cosh would give me a chance of winning this; I glanced about desperately for a suitable weapon as he closed again.

There was nothing. The hall had a row of pegs on one wall with some coats hanging on it, an umbrella stand with a feeble-looking lady's umbrella in it and a bentwood single chair. Nothing else. Crouching, I parried a right, blocked a kick and punched him hard on the side of the head. It made no difference. He landed a terrific right on the side of my jaw and then, just as the girl got the front door open and ran screaming into the street, he hit me, with a triumphant grin. It was a real purler this time, at criminal velocity. Apart from the sight of the hall lamp as it swung in an arc over my head and the interesting way the old-fashioned glass shade had an engraved floral pattern on it, I saw nothing else that I can remember.

CHAPTER 7

'Don't move,' the man in the white coat said. '*Ne bougez pas.* The ambulance is taking the *pauvres dames.*'

My face was wet. Putting my hand to it, I came across a damp cloth resting on my jaw, which felt as though it was broken but it wasn't. I worked it about a bit, wincing, and it cracked as things clicked back into place. I was half propped-up on a carpet in a sparsely-furnished room which I took to be the front of the house in the Rue Babie. It was bloody uncomfortable and I tried to sit up.

'*Non,*' the white-coated man said. 'You must be concussed.'

He disappeared and I noticed a uniformed gendarme standing across the room, looking down at me. Next to him was a youngish man in a dark grey jacket and lighter trousers, smoking. They both regarded me steadily. Putting a hand up, I felt for my wallet and papers in my inside pocket. They weren't there.

'I have your effects,' the smoker said. 'Who were the other two men?'

Beside me there was an armchair covered in rough moquette. I got an arm over it, a leg under myself and hauled myself into the chair. They made no attempt to help me but the white-coated man rushed in, clicking his tongue.

'I'm all right,' I said irrelevantly, in English. Sitting upright, supported properly, I felt better.

'Sit still,' said the white-coated man. 'We shall be taking you to hospital shortly.'

The smoker repeated his question. 'Who were the other two men? Where have they gone?'

I scowled at him. 'I haven't the faintest idea. Who the devil are you?' My head was starting to clear.

He exhaled some smoke. 'I am Inspector Dagallier, police. Who were the two men with whom you were fighting?'

'I have no idea. If you have filched my wallet and papers you will have seen that I am here at the invitation of Madame Boiteau to discuss a private matter.' I hunched over and drew up my knees. The blow to the stomach was sore and my jaw ached but I guessed that I had been out for only a few minutes, if that. A lot must have happened quickly. The sound of voices in the hall made me look up to see, through the open door, two white-coated men carrying out a stretcher. On it was a recumbent, blanket-covered form. Light flooded the hallway from the open front door as the first white-coated man came back into the room.

'*Alors, mon vieux*,' he said cheerfully, 'let's have a look at you.'

I let him peer into my eyes, feel my pulse. He nodded at

the two policemen. 'He's all right. But he must be taken for a check-up. It's the rule.'

The man who had called himself Dagallier nodded. 'OK. I'll bring him, don't worry.'

The ambulance man nodded and went out. I heard a vehicle start up and then there was a flash past the window as it pulled away. The plainclothes man offered me a cigarette.

'Concussed men aren't supposed to smoke,' I said grumpily.

He raised his eyebrows. 'You have experience? You are used to this sort of thing? Violence? Your card says you work in a bank. In what capacity?'

I sighed. 'This, I take it, is the response one gets in France for helping a lady who is being attacked? A grilling? You can check on my *bona fides* with my employers at the Bank and, if it is really necessary, with Inspector Roberts at Scotland Yard, who is a personal friend.'

He made a note. 'Such questions are most certainly necessary. You must agree that the circumstances are very strange. An old lady, obviously not rich, is attacked, tied up and suffers a stroke. A severe stroke. Her niece arrives home and is similarly attacked. The next thing she knows is that the hallway is full of fighting men, one of them a new one, well-dressed, but with the physiognomy of a pugilist. So I await your explanation: who were the other men and where are they?'

'The physiognomy of a pugilist? What the hell d'you mean by that?'

He held up a warning hand. 'I must warn you that my men are not enamoured of thugs who attack women. It is only professional restraint that has prevented you from getting a rough handling.' The French, in a crisis, can be very pompous and for a moment I had to observe him with amused detachment, even though he had obviously got hold of the wrong end of the stick.

'Dear God, Inspector, let me enlighten you. It goes like

this.' I explained the whole story to him, the first letter, the appointment, the Bank's interest, everything. He gazed at me, pursing his lips, especially at the last part, where I described charging in to help the girl.

'You did not know the man who answered the door?'

'No.'

'Nor the girl?'

'Of course not.'

Disbelief tinged his voice. 'You had no knowledge of this house or its topography?'

'None.'

He looked nonplussed. 'I am going to make some telephone calls. My men will take you to the hospital for a check-up and then to my office. This whole matter is very strange; perhaps you and these men, fighting over this—this sculpture, whatever—have coordinated your timing badly. Or by amazing coincidence.'

'Perhaps they were just thieves?'

He smiled mockingly. 'Here? In this house? Look at it—there's obviously nothing to detain a thief here.'

It was true. As they helped me to my feet and the uniformed gendarme led me out, it was clear that Madame Boiteau lived in very straitened circumstances. The place was clean but poor, without modern equipment or furnishings, almost belying the neat, trim exterior. Faded gentlefolk, I thought sadly, keeping up appearances. The street outside, in strong sunlight, heightened the contrasting suburban prosperity of the houses and apartments around it, even though there were still some small, modest villas of earlier years. Even they were very neat, well-kept. Only the deserted lot at No. 8, overgrown and neglected, with its high trees at the back, cast an air of mystery on the mundane residences around it.

At the hospital they took my pulse, shone a torch into my eyes, took my blood pressure, checked the bruises, X-rayed my jaw. It's happened to me before, after several memorable rugger matches. I let them do what they wanted, unresisting and obedient, until they nodded to the accompanying gendarmes and we clumped back to the police car. The driver, putting down his radio speaker, was positively affable.

'*Ça va mieux?*' he queried, smiling. 'Nothing serious, eh? We have to follow procedure, you understand. Inspector Dagallier has asked me to deliver you to him most carefully. Please relax.'

And blow me, it was all smiles after that, quite the special treatment. Dagallier got to his feet when we entered his office, waved his men away and offered me coffee, which I accepted. He even smiled warmly and offered me a cigarette again, which I refused: I haven't smoked since I was at school.

'Everything has been confirmed,' he said. 'I have spoken to your Bank who expressed anxiety about you and would like you to phone them as soon as possible. A Mr Jeremy White; is that correct?'

'Yes.'

'Then I spoke to Chief Inspector Roberts at Scotland Yard. He absolutely vouchsafed your integrity. Indeed—' he smiled for a moment—'it is now much clearer to me how your behaviour, which I found difficult to—explain, can be understood.'

'Oh, is it? How is that? What did Nobby Roberts say to you?'

'Please don't be offended. I understand that he is an old friend of yours and the, um, physiognomy—excuse me, the broken nose; from rugby of course, I should have known. But when I told him how you intervened in the attack on the girl he confirmed that your action was absolutely consistent. Indeed, he laughed; he said that Tim Simpson would never be able to resist a bull-like charge to the assistance of a fair lady.'

'Bloody cheek.'

He grinned. 'On the contrary, I think it was a compliment;

such gallantry is all too rare these days. It was your sense of initiative that misled me; few people would have entered the house in that way. I owe you an apology. You must have found my attitude very annoying.'

'Oh, that's all right.' He really was a very nice guy under the Gallic pomp. 'I suppose it's understandable. How is Madame Boiteau, by the way?'

He looked grave. 'Not very good. As a result of the attack by these two intruders she has suffered a severe stroke and her life is in danger. Her niece, Jacqueline Boiteau, is with her in hospital although she was badly shocked herself. While she was giving the alarm the two men got away in a van parked nearby. Fortunately there was a police car patrolling near the Avenue du Château and we were, there-fore, very quickly on the scene.' He put his hands in his pockets, took them out, looked at them and lit another cigarette. 'A question; I hope you will excuse?'

'Fire away.'

'Do you know who else she might have told about this—this work by Rodin?'

I shook my head. 'No. Only my superiors at the Bank knew about it from our end. I've certainly not told anyone; indeed, one keeps this sort of thing very quiet. Perhaps she —Madame Boiteau, I mean—tried some other potential investors as well, to test the market?'

He frowned. 'Apparently not. I have only interviewed her niece briefly, at the bedside, but she does not think so. Indeed, she knew nothing about the work at all herself. It was a complete surprise to her. She says that her aunt had never even mentioned it, ever. She has, by the way, lived with her aunt for many years and was brought up by her following her own parents' death in Algeria.'

'How very odd.'

'Truly. As you saw, it was not a prosperous household. One would have thought that she would have financed a better standard of living by its disposal at a much earlier date. What disturbs me now is the location of this piece, if it exists. I have ordered a search of the house for security reasons but the niece seemed very doubtful that anything could be found. She claims to know everything in the place, but of course a young woman might not be aware of how well the elderly can sometimes hide things.' He brooded for a professional pause. 'From your expert knowledge have you any idea how large the piece might be? Its dimensions?'

I shook my head. 'The Musée Rodin is the best place to ask that. I'm afraid I'm no expert on sculpture.'

'But you are responsible for such investments?'

'Oh yes, but I would have called in an expert for authentication of the piece. Naturally from auction records and expert opinion one would establish a price. To establish whether it were genuine—size, technique, patina, all that sort of thing—that's not my field. What would be very important would be the provenance, the direct line of attribution back to Rodin, who owned it, when, contemporary supporting evidence, documents, letters and so on.'

'Ah. There must be something somewhere. But we do not know what we are looking for; a bust, a complete figure?'

'Rodin produced both, of Gwen John.'

'In that case apart from searching the house there is little more we can do except wait for poor Madame Boiteau to regain consciousness. If she ever does. And if her brain is not impaired. Naturally we shall try to find the two men with the utmost effort but ...' He left the sentence unfinished. The chances of tracing the van, the men, depended on careful routine. There would be my description and the girl's and, as though reading my thoughts, he said, 'Are you staying in Paris long?'

'I've booked into an hotel in the Avenue Wagram for a day or two.'

'In that case I would be grateful if you could visit us again here tomorrow. To look through some photographs. What is it you call it—oh, I remember—a rogues' gallery. I will arrange transport. I think you should rest now. A car will take you in to Paris and bring you back tomorrow—say at midday so that you can have time to rest and I can assemble a suitable selection for the portrait gallery. OK?'

'OK.'

He bowed. 'Thank you. *A demain*; and take it easy, eh? No more *galanterie* for the ladies for a day or two.'

CHAPTER 8

'My dear Tim!' Jeremy's voice on the line was petulant. 'For heaven's sake! How on earth do you do it? This is precisely the sort of thing Sir Richard most wants to avoid. Every time you go out on a slightly unusual sort of errand for the Art Fund we get this sort of thing.'

'Jeremy, you've said "sort of" three times, which must mean—'

'Tim! Don't be flippant! This is serious, damn it. The old woman has been bashed to bits, you're obviously light-headed from concussion, and the whole project has become a liability. Here we are, starting on serious matters at the Bank, where I need you urgently, and you're lying half-silly in an hotel in Paris. I'm beginning to think that the Art Fund would have been best left with Geoffrey. At least the financial and industrial schemes we're looking at are solid, respectable matters. You always seem to get *involved* some-how. Now look here; there's no girl in it this time, is there?'

'Well actually, Jeremy, there is. I've not really met her yet but she's Madame Boiteau's niece, apparently. Quite pretty, if a bit plump, but then you know the plump ones are often—'

'Tim! I absolutely forbid it! You are *not* to get involved, is that clear? If it weren't for this police meeting you have to go to I would order you back at once. At once. As it is, you must phone me this evening, after you've seen them. Is that understood?'

'Yes, Jeremy.'

'And Tim?'

'Yes, Jeremy?'

'You are all right, aren't you, dear boy? I mean, well, you know, nothing serious, is it? Mary Waller took the incoming call from the Frog policeman and she was quite agitated; thought you were done for. She sends her best—you've obviously made a hit there.'

'Thanks. I'm all right, Jeremy. You know me.'

It was half past nine in the morning, the following day. I had slept very soundly from about nine o'clock the previous night until a maid brought me breakfast at half past eight. Beyond the long, old-fashioned net-curtained French windows the traffic on the Avenue Wagram outside rumbled cheerfully in the morning sun. My room was high, spacious, full of light. After a slow bath and shave I had phoned Jeremy at home, before he left for the Bank. I considered that I had earned my repose the night before and Dagallier had obligingly promised to send a message saying that I was all right but in need of rest.

The morning stretched before me, too good to waste. I read a paper, then I made a decision; I phoned Dagallier's office to cancel his kind offer of a police car, saying that I'd make my own way. Then I went downstairs and got a taxi, telling myself I'd earned the luxury of it this time. As the driver raced past the Arc de Triomphe, out towards the Porte Maillot to join the *périphérique*, I tried to imagine, yet again, what sort of a piece Madame Boiteau had on offer. Could it be a painting, or perhaps a sketch? My spirits fell at that. Rodin had done some painting and was a prolific sketcher. A study of Gwen John in pencil, or perhaps charcoal, would be delightful but not terribly valuable; a few hundred, perhaps a thousand pounds but not much more, not if it were just a working drawing. A fully-worked portrait

of her, now, that would be something, but no use for Sir
Richard's mysterious building foyer. I could justify buying
it for the Fund, though, and that cheered me up a bit. What
I really wanted was a bronze, a genuine contemporary
bronze, Rodin's work, at the time. I was interrupted in my
thoughts by the taxi-driver, who had raced round to the
south-west of Paris in no time and now wanted directions
to find the way.

'Villa des Brillants,' I ordered. 'Sentier des Brillants. It's
the local Rodin museum.'

Diamond villa. Meudon is a funny place to find your way
about, all piled up on the side of a hill, with no discernible
centre. It is largely residential, impersonal, devoid of the
bars and restaurants that automatically come to mind when
you think of a French suburb or town. You follow a sign
saying *Centre Ville* and find, before you know it, that you are
out on the other side. The taxi-man was in difficulties; we
had to ask our way several times before, winding through
cramped and steep streets punctuated by railway lines and
viaducts, we stopped, high up, by a set of gates at the end
of a short avenue of trees.

'*Violà!*' said the cabbie triumphantly.

I tipped him well, waved him off, and turned to enter.
That was when I got my first disappointment; the bloody
place was closed.

Open, a notice said, Sunday 1.0–6.0, Saturday 1.30–5.30,
and Monday 1.30–5.30. 1st April to 1st November only.

'Sod it,' I said, out loud, 'it's Tuesday.'

The Villa des Brillants in Meudon is where Rodin lived
towards the end of his life. He died there. It was, and is, a
tall, bright red brick, stone-edged box of a villa with a great
high spike of a roof punctured by sharp-gabled dormer
windows. Everyone thought it was inappropriate, vulgar
and actually cramped for the needs of a monumental sculptor, his assistants and his lifelong mistress, Rose Beuret.
Rodin was unabashed. He built workshops alongside, he

liked the view over the Seine towards Paris and he loved the garden, where he arranged his own and his collection of ancient sculptures. The temple and exhibition hall he moved there, a sandstone mock-Greek affair, was to house examples of his work. A large bronze Thinker crouches outside it, chin on fist, over the grave of Rodin and Rose, whom he finally married. I stared at it all in impotent rage. There is simply no consistency about the museums of the world, or even of one given country. They all open at different times, on different days, during different seasons. I was willing to bet that the main Musée Rodin, in the centre of Paris, had completely different opening hours.

Turning to my left, I walked down the great iron railings that bound the garden land, or what's left of it: a few cleared acres which must once have been formally gardened and full of interest. Going down the hill, staring in at the house across the wide green field around it, I tried to imagine it as it had been. Poor Gwen John, rejected in favour of the 'vulgar' red-haired American Duchesse de Choiseul, had crept round this same boundary, aching to get a glimpse of her lover, her master, the man for whom she wrote that she was the only true wife. At least when he was here, with the bad-tempered termagant Rose, he was not cavorting with some new conquest in his studios in Paris or in society. Very often she crouched in these grounds, seeking a sight of him, seeing the distinguished visitors like George Bernard Shaw and other men here for their portraits to be sculpted. Rodin was not unkind or cruel deliberately; indeed, he comes out considerately from many memoirs, but the number of his ladies and their passion for him beggars description. It was not only Gwen John who roamed these grounds and sank, later, into a religiously-obsessed decline. His famous pupil, sculptress Camille Claudel, suffered the same fate. Somewhere about the grounds I was looking at these ladies had wandered in despair; it made me stop and ponder.

The view over the river has been obstructed by railway

viaducts but I could see houses and villas on the other side, climbing the bank in close-knit domesticity. The gardens of the Villa des Brillants end in rubbish; a waste lot, strewn with papers above a factory yard filled with junk. At the other edge an extraordinary jumble of shacks, behind a paling fence, houses people, workshops and garages in a shabby corrugated tangle around a curious, oval, chopped-off cement building that may be the relict of a windmill. I stared at it in disgust. The sub-classical exhibition hall reared above me behind a high wire-mesh fence. The remaining bit of formal garden, hedged and pathed, with ivy clambering up the trees, could once have been entered from here below the house through a small wrought-iron gateway, now overgrown and fenced off. It was probably through that very gate, I thought, that Gwen John might have crept in her sad incursions to this place, as a child gazing into a lighted house at night might envy the adult celebrations within.

'Ghosts,' I said, out loud again, above the rattle of a distant train on the omnipresent railways. Somewhere around here she had sat in the bushes sketching the villa, her cat Tiger keeping her company. She would come out from Paris, not having yet moved to Meudon, and spend the day here, sunbathing and sketching. In those grounds, once assiduously gardened, had been a pool with some statuary, swans, a bench Rodin liked to sit on and survey the hilly, wooded panorama. I felt a sense of loss. Eighty years, almost, have passed since those events and yet to me it seemed quite recent, as though I could still somehow catch a glimpse of the protagonists right there at the scene. I tried to decide whether it was the recent freshness of my reading on the subject that made the place so vivid to me or the new violent involvement with the elusive object of Madame Boiteau's that had me committed, now, to pursuing what had been a casual goal to the very end, bitter or not. I suppose Sir Richard must have had a point when he

mentioned tenacity; I simply hate to leave a thing unfinished. The Villa des Brillants was a very suitable place
to start my quest, even though I could not get in and there
was no Gwen John in this, the territory of Rose Beuret. I
stuck my hands in my pockets and strolled thoughtfully
back down the hill through the town to the gendarmerie.
They greeted me warmly and Dagallier came out of his
office with a friendly grin to shake hands.

'How are you? Better? You look all right; a bit—what—
bemused, I'd say, it's normal after a blow like that. No
double vision? No problem focusing?'

I shook my head. 'I'm fine, thanks. But how is Madame
Boiteau?'

'Alas, no change. In a coma. It seems that she is in a
severe condition and her niece is very distressed. We have
searched the house without adding anything to our knowledge. Fingerprints are being analysed and I hope for some
results but we need a lead. It is likely that they will move
Madame Boiteau to a specialist hospital in Paris today, at
our indication of the seriousness of the situation. She is the
key to the whole thing.'

'Of course. I'm sorry I can't cast any more light on events.
You'd better show me your holiday snaps.'

He took me through to a small room with table and chairs.
On the table was a pile of large, bound folders. 'Sit down
here; take your time. I'll tell them to bring you a coffee. Just
leaf through until you see a face you think you know.
Mademoiselle Boiteau—the niece—will be doing the same
thing later but we need to be careful to preserve independence. Call me if you find anything. OK?'

'OK.'

I remembered an antique dealer I knew well on the
Brighton Road, an oldish woman who ran a very good shop,
having to do the same after a theft which she was sure one
of her shop visitors that day had committed. The Brighton
police brought her a similar set of photographs and asked

her to look. She got a shock when she opened the books.

'But these are all my friends!' she protested to the detective. 'The Brighton boys who call here all the time!'

Well, there were no friends of mine in the Meudon gallery. I leafed through slowly, gradually becoming saturated with faces, types, eyes and mouths. I paused after about fifteen minutes and closed my eyelids to try and clear my brain of the sea of faces. I thought of the man, half-hidden by the door, his dark surly face, the contemptuous jerk of the head. I thought of him as I landed that chop to the neck, the smell of him, the dark crisp hair, the black, straight eyebrows, powerful jaw, the one I hit to little purpose. Not a featureless type by any standard. Opening my eyes, I went on turning the pages. Five pages later I got him.

'Unmistakable,' I said to Dagallier, when he came in response to my call.

He sucked in his breath and put a cigarette back in his mouth, puffed and took it out again. '*Merde*,' he said.

I raised my eyebrows at him. 'What's up?'

'You certainly have picked a beauty.' He shouted through the door and two detectives came through. Without expression he pointed to the photographs of the black haired man. 'The friend of Mr Simpson,' he told them. 'His sparring partner yesterday.'

One of them stared at me. 'You are sure?'

'No doubt of it. That's the man.'

He whistled softly. '*Félicitations*.'

'Why?'

Dagallier grinned. 'My colleague is congratulating you. On being alive. This man is called Falco, or sometimes Falière. You are not the only lucky one. Mlle Boiteau has also been very fortunate. He has an extremely unpleasant way with the ladies. Extremely unpleasant.'

'Should I know him?'

'No, but we do. He is a professional. Algeria, Corsica, Marseilles, Paris, Lyons, even London. He is hired by various people. He is not supposed to be in France right now. He is supposed to be in Quebec, since eighteen months. This is now a very serious and interesting affair. People do not involve Falco for small reasons. He was arrested in Strasbourg four years ago and escaped, some said through influence from above.'

'You seem to know a lot about him.'

'Let us say that he is one of those that any policeman of a professional sort should know about. My colleagues here will, like me, have his name and details up here.' He tapped his head. 'We will now be able to check fingerprints from the house with particular care. Tell me, you didn't by any chance hit him—' he patted his chest on the left side, near the heart—'here, did you?'

'No, I don't think so. Why?'

'Because you would probably have broken your knuckles. He always carries a gun under that armpit, slung in his jacket. A big one, usually an automatic. He had no time to draw it out, obviously, otherwise you would not be here. You would be in the morgue. He is also a very skilled fighter and was, briefly, a boxer.'

'Was? He's not exactly retired now.'

Dagallier looked at me reflectively. 'He is known to have a sympathy towards the boxing world, his old friends. Perhaps he took you too for a member of that fraternity. He might just have swapped punches with you rather than more lethal blows for that reason.'

'Thanks very much.'

'Don't be upset. I have, no doubt that you are quite competent, quite useful in a brawl, but have no illusions; this is a real tough professional, an expert, a killer with his hands as well as his gun. Against such a man none of us here would do anything other than shoot first and ask questions afterwards.'

I nodded, thinking of the triumphant grin Falco had bared as he hit me for the last time. 'Seems I was lucky.'

Dagallier nodded, with a smile. 'Perhaps you may have reason now to feel less dislike for the incident which caused your own—er—'

'Broken hooter? There were never any hard feelings about that. I did it trying to score a try by going straight through a goalpost.'

He chuckled. 'Exactly. Well, to continue: have you seen the other man in the photos?'

I shook my head. 'No. I'll look through the remaining books, but nothing so far.'

'Good. We shall be issuing descriptions and the necessary alerts immediately. It is not good news for us.'

They trooped out, talking animatedly, and I went back to the remaining mug shots without success. The scruffy-looking man was in none of them. Dagallier arranged for me to make a statement and confirm the identification; he was confident, now, that they would find fingerprints to corroborate my evidence.

'Thank you very much,' he said, shaking my hand warmly on departure, 'and keep in touch, eh? There is nothing to detain you but we will let you know if Madame Boiteau recovers. Do you need a lift back into Paris? I will arrange it with pleasure.'

'Thanks. Just to my hotel.'

It was mid-afternoon and I might have done something else but I felt tired, so I just watched the streets of Meudon and then Paris roll past me as the police driver took me back. A sense of unease permeated my thoughts; I was only an incidental actor in the drama of the Rue Babie, not a principal; it was all a coincidence and there should be nothing for me to worry about. But I was worried and I felt tired and drained, distrait. When he dropped me off at the Avenue Wagram I thanked the driver cordially and went into the hotel, up to my room, to lie down. With the shutters half-closed and the calm airy height of the room to lull me, I soon fell into a doze, troubled by dreams of men fighting and a banging that stemmed from a mysterious source. Trying to throw the images off, I turned to put the dream away, flicking my eyes open, only to find that the banging came from someone knocking at the door. Straightening my clothes and slipping my shoes on, I opened it.

She was not quite so plump close up, but pleasantly plump none the less. She had changed her cotton dress and was in a blouse and skirt, but the leather handbag slung on her shoulder was the same one as I had last seen burst open on the floor at the bottom of Madame Boiteau's stairs. Her ample bosom and wide hips strained the blouse and skirt a little and she wore no make-up. With her upturned nose and soft fullness under the chin she almost looked like a country girl.

'Monsieur Simpson? Excuse me for disturbing you; I did not mean to derange but I have not had a lot of time and I understand you may be leaving soon. I wanted to thank you.'

Her hair was dark brown and, seeing it, I was disconcerted by the thought of Sue and her presence, full and feminine, in the doorway. I opened up a little wider.

'You must be Jacqueline Boiteau? I'm sorry—I had dozed off. Please come in.'

I stood aside to let her pass me but three-quarters through she stopped and peered at my face. 'Oh! How painful! Your jaw is badly bruised! I am so sorry, but so grateful—God knows what would have happened to me if you had not appeared. The police told me where you were staying and it was the least I could do to thank you. What courage! Those pigs! My poor aunt—she had nothing—why did they do it?'

Her eyes filled with tears. Her face began to tremble. Deeply embarrassed, I closed the door and steered her to an armchair, the only one in the room, and sat down myself on an upright dressing chair that I dragged out from under the mirrored table.

'How is your aunt?'

'Forgive me,' she wiped her eyes with a tissue handker-chief from her leather bag. 'She is still unconscious. They have no idea when she will recover, if ever she does. My God! My aunt is so dear to me—' she began to cry again —'more than an aunt, a mother, I have been with her for many years, since my own died—in Algeria—my poor aunt never had any children, my uncle was killed in 1940 so she took me in and loved me as a daughter. We have been so close; we had no one else. It's unthinkable. All of it.'

My life was suddenly invaded by this warm, wet, vibrant female with her generous figure, pressing her personal cir-cumstances, family life, feelings upon me as though I were not just a stranger who had lent a passing and ineffective hand to extricate her from yesterday's predicament. I was embarrassed, ashamed at my lack of response, feeling an English reserve well up to overcome any wish to participate I might have had. She was too—personal, that was the word—too open; not in control of herself. She should have telephoned me, I thought weakly, thanked me by phone call. This is too much.

'You know why I came to see your aunt?'

She rallied herself. 'Yes. The police told me. It was a bombshell. I had no idea. She never mentioned a thing to me, never. How could that be? Are you sure you have the right—?' She left the question unfinished.

'Do you want to see her letter?'

'Please.'

I got the letters out, the first one that had come to mind at the meeting with Sir Richard and the second, confirming the meeting.

'How strange! She never said a word. And I never saw your reply, although, of course, I usually leave the house before the post comes, to catch the train.'

'You work in Paris?'

She glanced at me quickly. 'Yes. I—I work as a receptionist. Or secretarial work. With an agency. It's difficult to get a permanent post just now.'

'I see. But you normally come to Paris every day?'

'Oh yes. We have to check in, to be available if a temp is needed somewhere.'

My thoughts were wandering on. 'Had your aunt lived in Meudon for a long time?'

'Since before the war.' She looked at me with a simple, guileless stare. 'She is quite old, you know, about seventy. When the war broke out my uncle was already away; they had only been married a year when he was called to the reserve. He got killed in the first German advance, towards Lille, before the capitulation. She was heartbroken. She lived alone, with her cats, like a much older woman, and was very poor; only a widow's pension. When my parents died she took me in. She wouldn't work but she looked after me and the cats on almost nothing. My father was in the army too; he was killed in Algeria with my mother, right at the end. We had no luck, my family; none at all.'

Old, unhappy, far-off things; and battles long ago. And not so long ago, nor so far off.

'Now look at my poor aunt; what could it mean? Did you tell someone about this Rodin piece?'

She blurted the question out, half-aggressive, half-defensive, staring into my eyes with an accusation that took me aback.

'He knew, you see, that beast,' she went on hurriedly. 'He kept saying over and over again: Where is it? Where is it? The Rodin? The Rodin? I didn't know what he was talking about, there's no Rodin in our house, we are so poor, always have been. It was horrible. He was so strong, like a gorilla, with those terrible black eyebrows and he grinned so horribly. The other one too; he said she's well rolled, let's —no, I can't tell you what he said. But what is it? Does it come from the Villa des Brillants? The Rodin Museum in Meudon?'

'No. At least, I don't think so. Your aunt was not very specific, you see, but she seemed very positive about this '*œuvre*' in her letter to us. We would never mention it to anyone else. Discretion is absolutely guaranteed with us. We would never do such a thing. That's why I feel that your aunt must have told someone entirely different.'

She was instantly contrite. 'Oh, excuse me! I am sorry. You must forgive me. I'm so distraught, my aunt in hospital, the dreadful attack—'

I hastened to intervene before there were further tears. 'Of course. You must be terribly shaken. Look here, can I get you a drink or something from the mini-bar here?'

'No, no—' she held up a hand. 'Nothing. So stupid of me. I must be going soon—visiting hours are over—'

I stood up, relieved. 'Just a small one?'

'No, really.'

'You have no idea—I'm sorry to harp on the subject, but before you go—what on earth it could be that your aunt might have had, of Gwen John, by Rodin? A drawing, perhaps, or some kind of small figure?'

She stood up too, close to me, looking anxiously into my face. 'No. Not at all. Have you any ideas? What else could there have been?'

I shook my head. 'A plaster figure. A bust. Terra cotta. Clay. God knows.' A thought struck me. 'Tell me; were you expected home yesterday, at about that time?'

She licked her lips, her face quite close to mine now. 'No. There was no work for me yesterday so I came home early.'

'By pure chance.' Expensive, I thought, to go into Paris for nothing.

'Exactly.' She put her hand impulsively on my arm. 'And I have not thanked you, not nearly enough, for saving me from those two. I cannot tell you what might have happened.'

The room became small as our two upright figures filled the space available, the clear bit of floor not occupied by the bed, the wardrobe, table, two chairs, one stiff and hard, the other a lounger, to lie back in.

'Oh, er, really there's no need. It was the very least I could do.'

She was a big girl, soft and full, now right in front of me, close, with a wistful smile and an intent, beady look that set my nerves quivering.

'Of course I haven't. You haven't given me a chance. You are so English, so reserved, such a gentleman. You do not try to take advantage of the situation, even though you must know that you are very—' she paused and gave me a half-amused flash of the eyes—'very masculine. After all, the least a girl can do when she's been rescued by a knight from a fate worse than death is to be—how do you say it in English—obliging?'

CHAPTER 9

'What a shambles.' Sir Richard White almost glared at me, his face taut. Above him, the cast-iron Madonna still held the cast-iron waving child out into the morning air, twenty feet up on its column, as though expecting a skyborne hand to lift it away. If she had dropped it there was a fair chance that it would have brained the Chairman of White's Bank below, staring at me in the misty morning light of the Dordogne river bank. I said nothing more; there was no point in getting all defensive about what had happened.

'You seem to have a talent for this sort of imbroglio.'

I refused to be drawn. Never complain, never explain; those Indian Army regiments had the right idea. It's all this modern business of communication, explanation, justification that spoils life. I knew that if I waited long enough he would simmer down and I could get on with the business I had with him. Jeremy had been quite jubilant on the phone

the previous evening, although he had complained of the
necessity of his ringing me instead of vice-versa, as I had
promised to do after my session at the police station. He
would have complained even more if he had known the
reason; I had to move the luxurious body of Jacqueline
Boiteau to one side in order to pick up the receiver.

'What a good thing that you're still in France after all!'

'Jeremy?'

'It's my uncle—Richard—he's getting the Bank into a
very hairy-looking scheme with a Frenchman. I don't like
it. I've got him to agree that you'll meet him tomorrow
morning, to go with him to the next meeting he has with
this man. I mean to say, a tissue factory, converting tissue
paper! What he really means is *bog rolls*, I suppose. Us!
White's Bank! It's most inappropriate. I think he's gone off
his trolley, you know. There's no other explanation for it.'

'I see. So you want me to stay here?' I glanced down at
the form beside me, the dark wavy hair, a modestly raised
knee. She smiled secretively. 'I've no objection to that, I
must say.'

'Good. You must be early. Eight o'clock. He's agreed
to meet you at a thing called the Talbot Monument. At
Castillon-la-Bataille.'

'Where?'

'For heaven's sake, Tim, will you listen? On the Dordogne. That's where he is. I told you; he has a house down
there but it's miles up river, inland. You've to be at Castillon
at eight tomorrow morning. The Frenchman's nearby.
You'll meet him.'

'Christ! That's near Bordeaux! At eight o'clock? For God's
sake, Jeremy, have you any idea how far that is?'

'My dear Tim! This is important! There are evening
flights down to Bordeaux from Paris. Get a taxi to the
airport, you've got bags of time. There's nothing to detain
you now, is there?'

'I—er—I suppose not.'

'Then for heaven's sake get on with it. You said that you were quite recovered yesterday. Haven't had a relapse, have you?'

'No.'

'Not got involved in any other shenanigans, have you?'

'No, er, no.'

'What?'

'I said no.'

'Good. Then off you go, and listen carefully to everything that's said. It's a very odd business to involve the Bank in. He's been keeping the whole thing right under his hat, telling no one. I found out—no, never mind how I found out—he won't be too pleased to see you, but he's had to agree. Especially in view of your—your incredible propensity for these involvements.'

'Thanks.'

I had to put the phone down, bitterly, and explain my departure to Jacky—her familiar name, you might say—who was extremely disappointed but understanding. I left the hotel as soon as I could, well, after what you might call a fond farewell, and everything went only too well for my journey south, leaving no chance of a conveniently-missed plane or anything like that.

Sir Richard, having me imposed upon him by Jeremy and exasperated by events in the Rue Babie, was once again making a passable job of accepting the situation. He moved a few paces away from the column, out of range of any falling iron infants, and looked at me with a little less acerbity. The sun was picking up and the trees on the other side of the river, with the vague outline of buildings among them, were shaking off the dew as a light breeze ruffled them.

'You really do seem to walk into the sprung boxing glove,' he smiled, conjuring up an image, doubtless, from the *Beano* comics of his youth. 'What on earth all that was about is incomprehensible and very disturbing. She must have put this—this Rodin piece about to other people; criminals have, quite clearly, got wind of it. This is most distressing and I do not like our being involved. But there you are—with art, particularly with associations like Rodin, one must, I suppose, expect an element of not just unconventionality but of Bohemian violence, extra-social mayhem. As you know, I've always had my doubts about the Fund.'

Doubts, I thought to myself, doubts, you old buzzard, you've done your damnedest to stifle it and everything Jeremy ever did at birth.

'Publicity is all very well,' he was going on, 'but discretion is the hallmark of the banking world. To be associated with all that sensationalism is not my idea of things at all. A quiet support to the Arts, patronage, the use of sculpture to alleviate the ersatz ugliness of modern buildings, that's another matter. Paintings in the right offices and board-rooms, perfectly acceptable—'

If, of course, they are nice conventional paintings with blue skies and calm seas or pretty women with dresses on amid flowers or a landscape with a horse and a farmer and a woman collecting a bundle of sticks—

'—but the racy element always attracts disaster. Now that I think about it, Rodin was a bit highly seasoned, wasn't he? Weren't there a lot of writhing figures in some of his pieces?'

'Um, well, some, Sir Richard. He rather took to idolizing the female form as a source of, er, artistic inspiration. His muse, so to speak.'

'Hm. Very French.'

No, I was about to disagree again, it could be argued that since Rodin was the son of an Alsatian woman and a Norman father his character was Saxon-Celt, but it depends on whether you believe in heredity or environment as a source of influence and I wasn't going to get into all that. Sir Richard seemed more relaxed, so I put to him a question which had, throughout my reading and background work, been plaguing me.

'Actually, there's one thing I don't understand about Rodin.'

'What's that?' The response was mildly encouraging.

'His first love was Rose Beuret and she had one son of his, called Auguste as well.'

'So?'

'Well, you would think, wouldn't you, with all those dozens, if not hundreds, of lady-loves, there would have been other children, bastards, somewhere, with at least one of them. Where are they all? They couldn't all have been hushed up, could they, because some of the ladies would have been proud about it. I mean, years and years of affair after affair, yet nothing. Why?'

'Syphilis,' said Sir Richard, promptly.

'I beg your pardon?'

'Probably syphilis. An older man would guess immediately. A lot of them had it. Rodin came from the Vaugirard slum district of Paris, in which it must have been endemic. Wasn't that son of his a half-wit?'

'Backward, perhaps; yes, I think so.'

'Well, there you are. It's obvious. It would have gone into remission, of course, so the contagion would have gone. They did have treatment in those days, mercury pills and so on. A lot of famous people had it, including royalty. Look at Lord Randolph Churchill. Yes, that would be it; in remission, but it would leave him impotent.'

Sir Richard's abrupt, older realism had set me back a bit; coming from him, it had an unexpected ring, like an off-colour remark from one's father. I hastened to catch up with my thoughts.

'Well, it's an interesting theory. I did wonder if, it being such an affair, Gwen John had not perhaps had a child or something.'

He turned his mouth down in a negative grimace. 'We should certainly have known if she had. Look at her brother. He used to say that when he walked down the King's Road he patted all the children's heads in case they were his own.'

You bloody old buzzard, I thought again, you careful fraud. Pretending, back in London, to be vague about art and sculpture; asking innocently-worded questions, humming and hawing. You probably knew more than I did about Rodin all the time. What the hell are you at?

'Yes,' he went on, stroking his chin, 'Augustus John used to have a theory that Willie Orpen died of it, although all the evidence points to drink. Anyway, it was a pretty regular and nasty feature of life before 1914.'

'Died out in favour of herpes now,' I said thoughtfully.

He shot me a look. 'I think we had better go steady on the question of the sculpture, temporarily anyway. If this Madame Boiteau recovers, then all can proceed. Keep alongside, would you? The project itself is much more important, of course; that is what we are here to get on with. It is of great significance to our future direction and policy. Tell me; don't be offended, but as we walk back to our cars, I would like to know what you consider the role of merchant banks to be?'

I turned carefully back towards the river, down the gravel path between the hedge and the roses towards the bank where the helpless retreat had foundered. It irritates me to be treated like that, made to be exposed and to reveal one's knowledge or lack of it, like a child put up to recite its tables. I was never the evangelical type. I managed to keep an even voice as we walked slowly along, side by side.

'The main function of the merchant banks is to raise capital for industry. They don't actually put it up themselves, they sponsor or underwrite share issues on the Stock Exchange. It's another form of gambling rather than participating in industry. Of course, the term "merchant bank" is hard to define; there are seventeen that belong to the Accepting Houses Committee, which is rather exclusive and of which we are not a member. Some of the smaller banks bear very little resemblance to the bigger ones and carry out much different sorts of business. Many of all kinds have strong foreign activities, like us. Some do investment advice, portfolio management, personal finance, like we do in Park Lane. Some do term lending, factoring, that sort of thing. Most of them view life from a sort of City Conservative Party outlook; they know nothing about industry, for example.'

'I beg your pardon?'

'Oh, don't get me wrong; I'm not a political animal. But your City Conservative, like many others, thinks of himself as a business man, which he is, but nothing to do with industry. The City is about land and gambling. It's all to do with finance, insurance, bullion, commodities, plantations, import and export, trading, yes, trading, that's it. Financing and lending, sure. But industry, production itself, rather than the financing of it, that's never been their forte.' I wondered if Sir Richard was guessing that my summary was angled, warning a little about an involvement in production. To some extent I was toeing Jeremy's line but keeping my thoughts open, waiting for the Chairman to explain. 'Factories are more for Whigs, liberals, Socialists, provincial Conservatives. A few merchant banks have taken equity in companies, but not much in industrial ones because they haven't the know-how to understand industrial management. Slater, Walker was an exception, I suppose, more like a French Banque d'Affaires, but look what happened there.'

His face shone. 'Where do you see White's in all this?'

'A bit of a hybrid. Some financing, some acceptance credits, portfolio management and still, of course, quite a lot of overseas trade and its associated finance. Timber in Brazil and the Far East. Plantations. Finding overseas partners for clients; I suppose the term lending side must have involved the Bank more closely in some customers' affairs.'

We had reached the cars and he put his hand on the grey roof of his Jaguar. I considered quietly the thought that he

must keep it in the Dordogne just for local use, to avoid
having to drive from England or to have to rent a car. What
I had been trying to do was to point out to him, gently, that
White's was no repository of industrial knowledge except
by glancing involvement here and there.

'For example, Sir Richard, the man who ships timber is
a long way from being a cabinet maker. Or even a pulp
producer. And a pulp producer is a long way from being a
—a bog-roll manufacturer?'

He smiled. 'Admirably put. I understand and take your
point. You did, however, just mention a "banque d'affaires".
That sort of bank, here in France, takes equity in industrial
concerns and plays an active role, at board level, in the
management. The Germans do much the same. Which
country, currently, do you think is more successful indus-
trially? Britain or France and Germany?'

'Well, the answer is obvious but it's not quite so
simple—'

His hand smacked the roof of his car with a crack that
sent a bank-strolling moorhen leaping into the river in
alarm. 'Change! We must change! And the banks have a
duty, a role to play that is vital! You mentioned the finding
of partners. We must help to seek out the right partners,
bring the technology, set up the new ventures. If it is not
available within the country it must be brought from outside.
The foreigners have been taking our ideas, exploiting them
commercially and selling the products back to us. We must
reverse the process. This project is a classic case for us to
start with.'

'Tissue?'

'Yes, tissue! You will learn all about it this morning.
Unless we actively seek out such new projects and work
hard at them, the lessons of this place may be taught us in
even more severe a form.'

He opened his car door and took another look round.
'Quite apart from the lesson of new technology defeating

the old, Mr Simpson, there is another one that we, as Englishmen, should remember. Particularly here.'

'Oh really, what's that?'

'Deprived of their French empire, forced back into their own small island, the English—no, the British—took to fighting among themselves. The outcome of the defeat at Castillon, my dear Mr Simpson, was the Wars of the Roses.'

CHAPTER 10

I've never been a great believer in the so-called lessons of history. As I followed Sir Richard's grey Jaguar back along the river bank to Castillon and out the other side on to the small road through St Mague towards St Etienne, I wondered whether this was due to a belief in the abrupt Henry Ford school of thought on the subject or to the more sophisticated reasoning of Karl Popper, and decided that, like the man speculating on a preference for one of his girlfriend's legs or the other, the truth lay somewhere in between. Sir Richard didn't drive very fast and I had time to ruminate as I drove along. It seemed to me that I was going to find myself with a conflict of interest. As Jeremy's henchman my first loyalty was to him in putting the boot into this scheme; as a member of the staff of the Bank I did have a certain responsibility to its Chairman. It wasn't only a question of Old Guard and Young Turk, or whatever the right phrase is; they were both valid points of concentration, of focus. Jeremy was inserting me into Sir Richard's project as his own pet ferret; Sir Richard, in his manner and approach, was indicating a space next to him as a personal disciple. It was going to be tricky, particularly as I felt, just then, some sympathy for Sir Richard's evident idealism.

The Jaguar passed through St Etienne into a cluster of villages east of St Emilion and turned off into the lanes

between St Laurent and St Christophe. Nothing but ruddy
saints' names labelled these vineyarded villages set out on
the gentle slopes, as though wine and religion had gone into
business together. From what Jeremy had told me, Château
Pavie was not far away to my left and I thought of him,
open bottle airing against his vehemence about stirring
things up at the Bank. Well, here I was, in the Côtes around
St Emilion, never having guessed that the association would
be occurring *in situ*, as it were, so soon.

Sir Richard pulled off the lane through a stone-pillared
gateway into a longish drive. On either side of us the serried
ranks of vines marched across the land, tiny clusters of
grapes already evident. In front of the house, in mellow ochre
stone with long shutters to the double French windows, he
stopped and I pulled in behind him. We crunched our way
on foot across the gravel towards the big front doors above
a wide gentle flight of stairs flanked by ornamental urns. As
we approached the doors opened and a man dressed in grey
trousers, white shirt and black shoes stepped out.

'Richard!' His greeting was familiar and friendly but he
glanced at me in surprise.

'Henry!' My companion pronounced the name the English way, not as Henri, and shook hands with him warmly.
They exchanged greetings while I stood aside in obedient
deference. It was clear that they knew each other very well.
Sir Richard turned to introduce us.

'Henry, I've brought one of our bright young men with
me this time and I must introduce you. Tim Simpson, Henry
Dechavanne. Henry, Tim Simpson.'

'How do you do?'

'How do you do, Mr Simpson? You've come to keep an
eye on Sir Richard, eh, while he tours the vineyards?'

I smiled. His manner was pleasant, controlled. Brown
hair topped a handsome head the same height as mine. His
figure swelled at the well-tailored waist as you would expect
a prosperous, château-owning Frenchman's to do, but he

looked healthy, well cared-for, upright. His blue eyes were bright. I put him at about fifty years old.

'No vineyard tour, Henry, as well you know. Mr Simpson is one of our, er, business experts. You see, it's an indication of how serious our interest in the project has become. I should explain, Tim—' it was his first use of the Christian name, implying, in front of Dechavanne, a relationship that surprised me—'that Henry Dechavanne is head of the Banque Dechavanne in Bordeaux.'

I feigned understanding and nodded brightly.

'Henry has been remarkably successful in creating a bank, during the last ten years, that is highly regarded in this region. It is an object lesson to we older, more traditional banks.'

Dechavanne smiled in pleasure at the compliment. 'Come, come, Richard,' he murmured, 'you old English bankers are no slouches, now are you?'

His English was perfect, almost without accent. Around the side of the house I saw the gleam of another Jaguar, a white one this time, like Sir Richard's. Anglophile Frenchmen are not uncommon in the Bordeaux area, of course, and there is the long historical connection, but he was almost copy-book. As though guessing my thoughts, he spoke to me.

'I should advise you that my name really is Henry, not Henri. My mother came to France from England and insisted on the Anglicized version. Of course everyone in France has always called me Henri, but to my—what should I call you, my half-fellows?—I use the English form.'

'I see. Tell me: is there any connection, in your name, with Puvis?'

He stopped and stared at me, his face bright with comprehension. Sir Richard, however, hastened to intervene.

'Mr Simpson—er—Tim, is the chief administrator of our Art Fund, the one I may have told you about.'

Dechavanne clapped me on the back warmly. 'Bravo

indeed! But how knowledgeable! You are, of course, referring to Puvis de Chavannes, the artist, the painter.'

'Yes.'

He laughed. 'No, alas, I don't think so. To be honest,
anyway. There was an old aunt of mine, one of my father's
sisters, who claimed that we descended from a cadet branch
of the same family. Personally I doubt it; we could never
find any evidence of it. But how quick of you—is French
painting one of your special interests?'

'Oh no, only in a general way. Puvis is well-known, of
course, to the modern student. He's out of favour now but
there was a time when he was very influential on the young
English artists who came to Paris. For example, Augustus
John.'

For a moment the whole face stilled; Sir Richard, still
anxious to smooth my entry, did not seem to have noticed
it. 'Tim here is quite the expert,' he prattled on pleasurably,
'not only in paintings. You must show him your collection
of porcelain, Henry, when we have got through our discussions; I'm sure he'd love to see it, eh, Tim?'

'Very much.'

Dechavanne smiled again, relaxed, the moment of still-
ness over. 'A pleasure; my little collection always gives me
delight and I am only too pleased to bore my visitors by
showing them over it.'

'Well, later then.' Sir Richard was still to the fore. 'We
have business to attend to first, have we not?'

'Of course; business first, as always. Come in.'

He led us into the big house—I somehow could not think
of it as a château, although that is technically what it was in
the wine trade—and I asked him, as we went through the
large hall, across a black and white marble-chequered floor:

'You must be Grand Cru here?'

'Oh yes. Not a Premier Grand Cru, not yet anyway, but
a Grand Crû. I bought this place five years ago; it was one
of a very few that come on to the market from time to time,

occasionally, and I was lucky to get it. It is quite well equipped now; would you like to see round?'

'I'd love to.'

He nodded. 'Then you must see that too, afterwards. Now, into my study; the vineyard office is outside.'

His study was a square, high, book-lined room about twenty feet across. A French *bureau plat*, or writing-table, stood towards one wall, with documents on it. Leather chairs surrounded another low table at which we arranged ourselves comfortably. On the table was a tray with a silver coffee pot and cups of bone china. Dechavanne leant forward and started to pour, talking cheerfully, his clear blue eyes flicking across from Sir Richard to me.

'Please excuse the informal approach; when I am here, rather than at the bank in town, I try to relax a little. I suggested that Richard and I meet here today because it is not so far down the valley for him, much better than going all the way into Bordeaux anyway, and, to be quite frank, it was not convenient for me to do so. My wife does not always agree; she has gone into town to do some shopping.' He handed us our coffees, passed the sugar over and looked at me, poised. 'So tell me—what do you know about the absorbent tissue business?'

It was not aggressively put but it was a challenge; I felt him concentrate upon me, his body turning to face me square on.

'A little; as it happens, I once had a client who was in the business in a small way. But not here; it was in Brazil.'

'Really? Did you live there?'

'Not for long, I'm sorry to say.'

'Aha, you're obviously fond of Brazil, like me. A great country with great opportunities, which Richard and I have discussed. And a very good source of cheap soft tissue, Brazil, as it happens, like many paper products. But not by dry forming. Do you know what it means, dry forming?'

I glanced at Sir Richard, very irritated. He had not helped

me at all. No prior advice, no briefing; the penalty of being Jeremy's man and 'expert', I assumed. Well, OK, Sir Richard, if that's the way you want it. I gave Dechavanne a warm, insincere smile.

'Very roughly. Normal paper processes require vast amounts of water to suspend the pulp fibre in before it is drained on the machine wire and then formed and dried into paper. In dry forming you take the dry pulp sheet or roll and defibre it direct, without water. You form it on a wire by suction and you bond it like a non-woven fabric or just compress it or something. In fact most dry forming is used for producing non-woven fabrics.'

'Very good! Actually it is still quite complex. The original idea goes back a long way but in Western Europe now it originates with a Finn followed by a Dane called Karl Kroyer. Many companies have started in this field with a Kroyer licence. The big advantage is that you do not need the water, as you say. But for the moment the process is still very expensive to set up—less than normal paper processes, but millions are involved—and it is used for the heavier and more luxury end of the soft absorbent tissue market. Paper towels, for instance, and handkerchiefs. The machines are very big, like paper machines in a way. A lot of research and development effort has been involved, so naturally it is the Americans who have been much in the forefront.'

I nodded. 'American or Scandinavian, like the development of most tissue products. In the United Kingdom all the major producers are American or Scandinavian with British companies having, perhaps, a joint venture share. Otherwise there are only small units, old cellulose wadding machines—'

'Exactly!' Sir Richard leant forward, eyes ablaze. 'American and Scandinavian! Otherwise, older technology.'

'Well, it's not surprising, Sir Richard, pulp technology tends to follow the existence of very large forests, particularly softwood forests.'

He waved my remarks aside. 'There is no dry forming unit in Britain. There we go again. Instead of importing raw materials and converting them to finished products of much higher value, we have become a target for export-anxious foreigners with finished manufactures.'

'The UK is quite an efficient producer of tissue, Sir Richard—'

'By the old methods!' His interruption was brusque. 'Let Henry continue.'

Dechavanne smiled at him tolerantly. 'As I have said, dry forming is still a large, expensive process. There have been companies working on it for years who have spent very heavy sums of development money. Like so many paper mills, the economics of scale keep increasing so as to keep down production costs. A lot of mills have invested heavily in plant to process waste paper for tissue, with de-inking and all kinds of cleaning processes. It is very capital-intensive, unlike the converting processes, in which the equipment is relatively cheap.'

'The dear old Ozo-Soft Toilet Tissue Company?'

Dechavanne laughed. 'You have been to business school, too? That old Harvard case study must have been worked on by every student of business I ever came across. Yes, precisely that.' He was warming to me, a common bond being established by my remark, which had been carefully inserted. I guessed that he was a fine persuader, using the attraction of his personality with judgement to gain support and having, behind the use of that skill, a quite cold and detached view of the person opposite as his raw material to be influenced. All great persuaders and salesmen are the same.

'But imagine,' he went on, 'if, instead of these huge tissue plants, producing tens of thousands of tons, there was a small, lower cost alternative; a means of taking pulp, dry, and converting it directly into tissue at a narrow width—say up to one metre—and then converting that, perhaps even on the same line, into finished products? Towel roll or handkerchiefs or napkins, perhaps even toilet tissue? Can you imagine? If such small-scale industries were efficient, with local distribution, they would turn these huge, polluting white elephants of river-fed mills into the dinosaurs they ought to be. A measure of a country's economic development can be taken from its consumption of paper, particularly tissue paper. Yet here we are, in the advanced countries, distancing ourselves from everyone else and from reality by these vast juggernauts. A brand new tissue mill, using current technology, costs over one hundred million dollars to build. Imagine again: the sort of small cost-efficient plant I am talking about can be set up anywhere, in the Sahara if need be, but in many developing countries where water is very short and capital difficult to obtain. The potential would be enormous.'

His face was enthusiastic, practised; Sir Richard's was rapt. I ignored the inapt dinosaur comparison; the dinosaurs were a very successful species and lasted rather a long time, longer than we have, anyway, and concentrated on his careful use of words like 'can' instead of 'could'.

'Does this small unit exist, then?'

'No, of course not. But it is nearly there.' He leant forward. 'I know that you will treat this with the utmost discretion. On a laboratory scale the thing almost exists; defibration of dry pulp in hammer mills is a long-standing technology. Forming of the separated fibres so that they link without a bonding agent is the big step to carry out efficiently on a small scale. It is almost there; we have been financing a local technologist and his team in this for some time. The results are tremendously satisfactory at the higher weights, the thicker tissues. Where we need to work more is on the lighter tissues, the more commercial weights. But it is coming. What we must do is to set up a converting plant, a traditional tissue-converting plant for all standard commercial products, using normal jumbo rolls of tissue bought in from existing producers. This establishes a basic market without exciting suspicion.'

'But—'

'Wait, wait! Let me finish. To do it the other way round would be hopeless. If we went to converters with our dry-formed tissue to sell in rolls everyone would know immediately. If, on the other hand, we set up the conversion plant, we would steal a march on everyone. What is more, once having set up such a plant and shown, successfully, how an existing small converter could quite easily do the same, we could use the plant as a demonstration unit to sell the process and the equipment all over the world. We here would cover the French-speaking areas while White's would cover the Anglo-Saxons and your traditional trading areas.'

He sat back triumphantly. Sir Richard's eyes glittered. 'You see, Tim, we have been working on this project, Henry and I, for a long time. It is the kind of joint development ideal for us both and a model for the sort of project we must instigate. We shall finance it jointly. We have chosen a development area in Europe for the first, normal converting plant which will arouse little or no suspicion and attract very useful incentives to lessen the cost. The forming technology research will continue here in France and then the first production unit will be set up without fuss to produce for the converting plant, inside that plant.'

Dechavanne smiled his assent. 'It was a fortunate wind that brought Richard to the Dordogne. We have known each other socially for a long time but in the last few years we have often chatted about collaboration on modern industrial projects in an Anglo-French context. There is no doubt that we must pool our resources more and more, across EEC borders, if we are to survive in the industrial world against American and Japanese pressures. For Britain and France this is a logical, an ideal approach with our complementary skills and markets.'

Anglo-French collaboration, I was about to say, has a less than distinguished record from the Crimea to the Concorde, but Sir Richard was nodding like a toy dachshund in the back of a Cortina. Well, well, I thought, I've been allowed along for the ride and I've been given the courtesy of having the story from the horse's mouth, but you, dear old Uncle Richard, are very committed to this. What is more, you are either hoping I'll be out of my depth and make a fool of myself, or you're setting me some sort of test, or you don't give a bloody stuff what I say. Otherwise you would have briefed me properly. This very smooth Anglo-Frenchman has got you in his pocket over this; there have been no dimensions yet, no figures. They will be my job and Dechavanne will know it; assuming, that is, that you and he will divulge them correctly.

'This is clearly a very important project,' I said pompously, 'which requires complex analytical assessment. I assume—'

'Of course.' Dechavanne took my coffee cup and refilled it smoothly. 'We have done many feasibility studies, using computer models and the latest industrial statistics. I'm sure you know that the paper business is very difficult, very technical.' His face took on a muscle-bound look, the sort of look that men use at committee meetings where they have to put up a semi-public performance before the adoption of a pre-arranged decision. It was uninvolved with me on this issue; I was a squeaker of Sir Richard's to whom a gesture must be made. Dechavanne would be a man whose mind had clear compartments, concentrations, the ability to isolate one problem from everything else, like all businessmen of his type. To it would be added the advantage of a logical French mental discipline and the ability to conceptualize, to use the broad-brush intellectualism that is so admired in France. He would use that conceptual approach to put opportunities from different spheres of business together and create the even greater profit. Somewhere the use of White's

Bank fitted into the pattern in his mind but what that pattern was, outside of his explanation, would never emerge. I decided to go into reverse very quickly and take a pragmatic, Anglo-Saxon approach.

'I'm sure it is. Very technical. It's not necessary, in this case, to worry about that, though, is it?'

He gave me a tolerant smile, the sort of smile an adult fronts to a precocious child who has made a challenging statement of easy logical demolition. 'Really? You think we do not need to consider the technical aspect?'

'Not from an investment point of view. There are two simple issues: one, does the conventional converting plant you propose offer a reasonable return using normal commercial tissue; and two, the whole dry-forming project. Number two has, in turn, two aspects: technical and commercial feasibility. The fact that the conventional converting plant *might*—at some future date—be supplied by the new dry-formed material with its cost or quality advantages is a totally different matter.'

Sir Richard intervened quickly. 'That's not the way we see it. The two issues are not separate at all. The converting plant is quite simply in the vanguard of the project but it is integral with it and an important part of its strategy.'

'None the less—'

'None the less nothing!' he snapped. 'Let us be quite clear on this! Dry-forming technology is an accepted modern method of production and we shall be in the forefront of it. In a European sense. It's time that we took the initiative back from the Americans. No one doubts the use of dry forming; it's already used extensively.'

'In non-wovens maybe, Sir Richard, but in paper it has a limited use so far.'

His lips set in a line as he brought his teeth together. 'The use of the dry-forming technology is not an issue for debate! We are neither of us competent to judge! Results are what will speak for themselves and samples of sufficient quality and weight have already been produced.'

'By laboratory methods?'

His teeth practically ground together this time. He opened his mouth to speak but Dechavanne got there ahead of him. 'By laboratory methods, true, Mr Simpson, but they are methods which can be scaled up without problem and which do not depend on any esoteric technology. I rather think that Richard and I are too far down the line to wish to backtrack on this, but I am sure that you can be provided with sufficient information to satisfy yourself. We have some more developed aspects to discuss.'

So pipe down, Simpson, and try to catch up by doing some bedtime reading, there's a good boy, while the grown-ups keep going on ahead faster than your little legs might go. I was going to have to be quick; my mind was finding it all very difficult to grasp, all at once anyway, so I threw in a question, just to keep the pot boiling while my brain caught up.

'Where had you in mind for the conventional converting plant? The development area you mentioned?'

Sir Richard picked up his coffee with the air of a man who has just overcome a tedious interruption and is relieved to have seen it off. 'That wasn't difficult. There are a lot of areas trying to lure business ventures of any sort into them just now, using EEC funds. One of the most attractive at present is Wales.'

'Wales?'

'Yes, Wales. As a matter of fact, we have earmarked a very suitable site with enough space for expansion at Carmarthen. There is already a tissue mill at Bridgend— half Finnish—so we shall use their tissue to start with.'

'Good God.' My voice sounded far-off, incredulous. 'Carmarthen. How very, very appropriate.'

It was all starting to click into place now.

CHAPTER 11

I caught a direct flight from Bordeaux to Heathrow and thanked my luck that I hadn't left my car at Gatwick. There was no reading of poor Madame Boiteau's letter on the return flight; my mind was teeming with too many other impressions and events. The Rue Babie; the punch-up; Dagallier and his companions; Sir Richard and Dechavanne; most pleasant of all, Jacqueline Boiteau, or Jacky, as she had preferred me to call her.

There was an unreal quality to that interlude in my hotel room. It's not in my nature to look a gift horse in the mouth and she had been not only quite insistent but also extremely forthcoming. Indeed, I had an uncomfortable feeling that she had taken the initiative in a cool practical way that had made me a slightly secondary figure. She accepted my hurried departure, my profuse apologies, quite calmly. We agreed that we should meet again but that timing would depend on the condition of her aunt. There was no urgency or sense of responsibility about it. She had a quality about her that slightly depressed me; a stoicism combined with a vulnerability that perplexed my wish to understand her. Somehow she didn't seem to fit. Anyway, there had been little time to investigate this unease; my dash down to Bordeaux had seen to that. Just one of those hands, I thought rather complacently to myself, that life deals out to you, when in a benevolent mood, in return for a fit of timely bravado.

I took the Tube from Heathrow to save time and got off at Earls Court so that I could walk down Redcliffe Gardens through the square towards the Fulham Road. It was a slight comfort to know that, very shortly, I would be able to stay on the Piccadilly Line and get off at South Kensington because

I had agreed, before leaving for Paris, to buy a place in Onslow Gardens so as to be nearer the line. And, of course, to be in a more pleasant street with somewhat better social implications now that I had become a City gent. Who knows, I thought, I might meet a really with-it bird in this area, someone whose daddy would have a country place and all the trimmings; Jacky is hardly a firm engagement and Sue, well, the less said about Sue the better. All the same, it made me sad to think that I would not be in the Fulham Road place much longer. I had had some good years in it, one way or another, despite the painful memories. As I put my key in the lock I felt a pang of regret at the thought that I would not have to struggle with its erratic mechanism in future. I didn't have to then; the door was open.

They had done the place over properly.

The burst sofa was even more erupted than usual; papers from my fall-front bureau were strewn everywhere; books had been tipped out of the shelves; the carpet had been pulled out and turned back. As my gaze, stunned with shock, took in these immediate impressions, I started to absorb the detail: the paintings and sketches on the walls tilted crazily or hurled to the floor; drawers sagging open; ornaments and personal things swept off surfaces and strewn about; a curtain hanging askew, pulled off the rail. In the kitchenette the crockery was jumbled in a smashed shambles and a carton of milk lay on its side in a white-grey pool. I found a bottle of whisky with about one-third left, poured myself a glass and went into the bedroom; it was even worse. They had tipped the double bed over on its side, pulled out all the drawers in the chest and emptied them, taken everything out of the wardrobe and piled it on the floor. My shoes tangled under my feet; even my suitcase, the big one I use for long trips, yawned its open jaws at me to show its ripped lining. I sat down on the bedroom chair and drank the whisky, reflecting that I had a reserve, duty-free bottle with me too.

'Bastards,' I said, out loud.

Living in the Fulham Road, it's meant to be a local hazard, getting burgled, but it had never happened to me before. I'd never bothered much about locks and safety devices. I don't collect silver or jewellery, my paintings are Slade School British mainly, and I never have much cash about. If professionals want to clean a place out, they will; I had always figured that I didn't keep much for the general mass of part-time burglars, kids on the smash, that type. I felt as if someone had kicked me in the cods.

I went back into the living-room and stared hopelessly at the mess. Then I kicked the burst sofa back into position and took a look at the important things, like my hi-fi, which was still there. So were all the tapes and records. So was my spare cassette radio and the television set.

'Odd,' I said, out loud again, just as Sue Westerman walked in through the front door.

'Tim? The door was open and—oh my God! Oh, Tim! How awful!' She stood just inside the door, wearing a lightweight summer suit in beige weave, a cream blouse and a sort of satchel-handbag, slung over her shoulder. Her eyes stared in horror at the scene.

'Welcome to Simpson Grange,' I said bitterly, waving my glass in a grand gesture round the room. Nothing spilled from it because it was empty.

'What on earth has happened?' She took out her horn-rims and put them on, as though her eyes could not believe it.

'I seem to have been burgled,' I said. 'Or, as the Americans would say, burglarized. A common London experience, I'm told, but this is my first time, as the ladies always say. I have just arrived home to find—this. How are you, Sue?'

'Oh, Tim, how dreadful! I am sorry. I—I really am. Is there much missing?' She seemed to be genuinely upset.

'I haven't had time to check. Doubtless, as I go through, I'll find out. I haven't seen anything yet. Perhaps some kids were just having fun. Have you come to return something to the morass or to claim something you left? I thought you cleared out pretty thoroughly when you went.'

She frowned and bit her lip. 'No, I—I had to see you.'

'Really? Won't that upset Arthur? I mean, he won't like the idea of you visiting the apartments of old gentlemen friends on your own, will he? Especially drunken rugby players whose sole thought is to strip off—'

'Tim! Stop it!' A bit of her old schoolmistressy tone came into her troubled voice.

'Sorry. Would you like a drink?'

'I—I rather think I would. This is such a terrible sight. It's somehow much worse than I'd imagined coming back here would be.'

I went into the kitchenette and found that most of the bottles were intact.

'Gin and tonic?' Her usual tipple.

'Yes. Er, yes, please.'

She was perched carefully on the edge of the sofa. Her big spectacles glinted owlishly at me. When I gave her the drink she took a deep draught and then sipped, watching me as I picked up this and that, gradually straightening things.

'I came because I couldn't leave it the way it was,' she said, looking into the glass.

'Oh?'

'You were so upset. I've never seen you so upset. But you did infuriate me, you know. You always did. And that time —it was too much.'

'Yes. I'm afraid I was a bit, um, coarse. It was a shock, you see. Meeting you and then, well, Arthur.'

She was silent. I found that the still-life by Allan Gwynne-Jones was all right. So was the sketch of a soldier by Orpen. It wasn't an art burglar, obviously. The glass on the watercolour by Stanley Spencer was smashed, though.

'Damn,' I said, carefully picking out the splinters.

'Oh, Tim. They say you never feel the same about a place once you've been burgled.'

'I know. Fortunately I haven't got long to go.'

'What? You're leaving?'

'Yes, I'm moving. Onslow Gardens. In two weeks' time.'

'Oh.' Her voice was small now, tiny.

'Bit more salubrious, eh? Better class of burglar they'll have, over there. Time to move on. You know what I mean? Waking, dear, I see thee not, and all that.'

A dreadful, silent tear ran down her cheek. Then one went down the other side. More followed; it was appalling, heartrending; I could have kicked myself.

'You—um—you better let me hold your specs. Do you want to borrow a handkerchief?'

She shook her head. I reached out carefully to take the specs. It used to be a joke with us, or rather with me, about her specs. They were purely defensive, I used to say, a sort of armour that had nothing to do with her vision. Get Sue's specs off, I used to banter, and the rest of her gear is bound to follow. Now I held them cautiously while she dried her eyes, blew her nose and put them hurriedly back on.

'I'm all right, you know,' she said, in a tight voice. 'It's just this—this—' She gestured at the pillaged rooms.

'Would you like another drink?'

'No, thanks. Look, let me help you to clear up?'

'OK. If you'll do the kitchen, I'll do the bedroom. Arthur could hardly object to that, could he?'

She smiled faintly. I put the bedroom more or less back in order but there was to be another emotional crisis. In the kitchen she found a pretty yellow lustre jug she had once given me smashed to bits. She kept the specs on but she gulped Oh Tim again as she swept the glinting yellow and silver shards into a dustpan.

'Well,' I said as brightly as I could when we had finished. 'Thanks very much. I, er, I'm sorry about the other day. As I said, I was upset and—'

'I didn't only come about that.'

'Oh?'

'Tim, I can see the bruise on your chin. I know all about it.'

'You do?'

'I met Geoffrey last night in Hampstead.'

'At a party? Get around, you and Geoffrey, don't you? Was Arthur there?'

She ignored the response. 'He told me that he saw Jeremy and that you had been getting into trouble again.' Her eyes probed mine. 'Tim, what are you going to do?'

'Well, nothing, Sue, it's all in the hands of the French police; just a coincidence, you know.'

'Tim, don't insult my intelligence. You're always getting involved in these terrible situations. You seem to attract them. I fear for you, really I do. All your friends do. Don't try to pretend; I know what happened while I was away in Australia.'

'You do?'

'Yes I do! You got involved with some dreadful American vamp and—'

'Vamp? Vamp? Great heavens, Sue, there haven't been any vamps since the nineteen-thirties, you can't use words like vamp in—'

'Don't interrupt! You know what I mean! She shot you! I've heard all about it! You seem to have no control over your life; it's so shaming to have people look at me and know all about these things.'

'But you'd gone! You were in Australia. You left me.'

'Because it was such a good chance for me! You never would accept that, would you?' She sniffed. 'You could have stopped me, if you'd really wanted to, anyway.'

My jaw dropped open. I'll never understand women, never. She was absolutely hell-bent to go to Australia; I remembered it clearly. Would I have made a mistake over a thing like that?

'Look, um, Sue, this isn't getting us anywhere. I'll tell you what, I'd better drive you home, it's getting late.'

'All across London? Don't be silly. I can get the tube.'

'To Hampstead? From here?'

'Well, a taxi, then.'

'Rubbish. I won't hear of it. My car's just round the corner. It's no trouble, really it isn't. Besides, London at this time of the year is full of the most unsuitable tourists, foreigners of all kinds. You'll be pestered.'

I took her arm firmly, to escort her to the door.

'Wait! I brought you these.' She opened the satchel hand-bag and took out some papers, lecture copies, things like that. 'You wouldn't let me at the Tate, you were in such a state. About Gwen John. And some things on Rodin. Articles and stuff from our records that you won't find elsewhere.'

'Oh, great. Thanks, Sue.' I put them in the bureau and smiled at her. 'Don't worry, I'll make sure that they move with me.'

'You must tell me all about it; this thing you're after. Geoffrey says it's the cause of all the trouble. I didn't know that you liked Gwen John's painting; usually it's a feminine taste.'

'Actually, I have mixed feelings about it; the later stuff is problematical to me. Women love the story of her life and everyone who comes across her feels somehow involved; few people can resist the idea of the starving genius in the attic. The method of painting—thin glazes and so on—is said to owe a lot to McEvoy and Whistler but it really suits her own rather obscure qualities. Whatever you think of her brother, you can't simply say that she was a better painter, as some people now do, parroting his own remarks. He's out of fashion now but he was quite something; they were different, not to be compared. It's false to do so. It's her story and the deliberate choice of obscurity that fascinate everybody. More than her painting.'

'Perhaps you're right.'

She was looking at me in a much more composed way and so I told her, as I walked her to the car, about all the bits that had happened, except the episode with Jacky of course, but about Castillon and Dechavanne and Carmarthen. She got into the car quite excited by it, and all the way across London, round Regent's Park and on up to Hampstead, she chattered away happily about Rodin's contact with England, how he was appreciated here much more than in France to start with, and his helping Legros over, and how Whistler got involved and helped Legros to the job at the Slade. Then when Rodin sent his plaster model of the proposed monument to Whistler years later, for approval, with its muse for which Gwen John had posed, the committee didn't like it. The model disappeared and they thought it had never been found.

Then she talked about Gwen John, things I knew mostly already, her life in France and how she came back to England twice, once to the New Forest where Augustus tried unsuccessfully to get her to settle in a cottage and the other time, when she visited the critic and poet, Arthur Symons, at Wittersham.

A cold chill went down my spine. 'Wittersham?'

I had a sudden vision of the old sea cliffs at Wittersham, now land-locked, and the beautiful American, Marianne Gray, beside me in the car, the same car, in the passenger seat Sue was now sitting in, the one that tilted back so conveniently. Then I shut out the memory, too painful to dwell on. We had arrived at Sue's front door and I got out.

'Oh, I—'

Her excitement suddenly subsided. The flush died from her cheeks as though she had remembered something that blotted out the pleasure of involvement in the story. She put both hands on her bag and held it in front of her defensively as she spoke.

'Tim, I—'

'It's all right, Sue.' I stared at the passenger seat as I

opened the door for her. 'I'm just seeing you safely to the door. No panic. Nothing to worry Arthur.'

She looked down at the pavement and bit her lip. 'He doesn't get back from Melbourne just yet. You do understand, don't you? I'm sorry about the old flat.'

'Yes. Well, never mind. Change is inevitable. Thanks for the help, Sue. And for the articles.'

She stood, still hesitant, on the pavement.

'You'd better let me see you go in, just in case you've been burgled, too.' I stood back a pace and looked at the door, waiting. She nodded quietly, and put her key in the lock. Our eyes met. Then she disappeared through the door, out of sight.

I got back into the car cursing and drove back down into Camden Town blaspheming the whole way. The only thing that diverted my mind from the stupidity of life, my wretched emotions, and the bad hand I'd played was the thought of what an odd burglary I'd had. The only things that were missing were my books on Rodin and Gwen John.

CHAPTER 12

Nobby Roberts cut a piece of fried bread from the slice, put a half-rasher of bacon on it, put a liquid chunk of fried egg on top of that, topped it with a quarter of hot tomato and speared the lot savagely with a fork.

'Appropriate?' he growled irritably. 'What the hell d'you mean, appropriate?' He shoved the forkful into his mouth, working the lean fair jaw rapidly enough to make a lock of sandy hair fall across his brow as he kept his head down. Dark circles bruised his eyes. Having raided an antique dealer's store in Peckham Rye that morning before five o'clock, along with four of his plainclothes men, only to find that the huge pantechnicon van loaded with stolen goods had already left for the coast, he was not in a good temper. Calls to alert Dover, Folkestone, Newhaven, Southampton and Harwich had been put out; there was a faint chance that patrol cars might pick the load up. All he could do now was to wait; his nerves showed it.

Outside in Victoria Street the eight o'clock traffic was building up towards office hours. Breakfast in the Italian café to which I had lured him was always good value and it was near enough to his office in New Scotland Yard for him to find it acceptable on a working day. I hoped that his temper would improve as the breakfast progressed. So far he had not behaved very warmly towards my other guest, languidly dealing with scrambled eggs on the other side of the table.

'I think what Tim means,' said Charles Massenaux of Christerby's, carefully flicking a crumb from his perfectly-cut pinstriped lapel, 'is that Carmarthen has certain associations which would make it an ideal site for a Rodin statue of Gwen John in an Anglo-French factory.'

'Correct.' I nodded.

'Such as?' Nobby spoke with his mouth full.

'Well, as I recall, but correct me if I am wrong, Tim, it was in a car park in Carmarthen that Augustus John and Dylan Thomas had a punch-up over Caitlin McNamara, now Caitlin Thomas?'

'Absolutely right.' I smiled to myself as I thought of my reaction to the site when I was at St Emilion and how Sir Richard had had to explain the whole business and my bruised jaw to Dechavanne. He appeared to be very embarrassed about it and dealt with it as quickly as possible while I accepted Dechavanne's sympathies.

'It was a funny business, that, wasn't it?' Charles looked at me curiously. 'I mean, John thought of her as part of his own harem in a way, despite her being his step-niece. She spoke with distaste of his chasing her round the studio during modelling sessions. But then John always chased his models round the studio, no matter who. He seemed to think that his reputation demanded it. So did Rodin, in a more gentlemanly way.' He finished off a little scrambled egg carefully before taking a sip of black coffee. 'On the other hand, to be charitable to John, it is possible that Dylan Thomas had confided to him during their drinking sessions that he had caught a dose of the clap and that John simply wanted to protect Caitlin, knowing that Thomas fancied her.'

Nobby paused with another forkful of cholesterol on its way to his mouth and I shifted uneasily in my seat. It's odd how certain themes, once started, seem to pervade life for a bit. 'Do you mind? We're having breakfast.'

'Sorry. Thought you two ex-rugger men had strong stomachs.' The Christerby's man smiled blandly, his long face under the thick smooth hair remaining unemotional, undisturbed, as only a man who deals constantly with the disposal of personal possessions at auction learns to do.

I finished my own bacon and eggs and signalled the Italian waitress for more coffee all round. Nobby began to tuck into toast, grimacing at the plastic sachets of marmalade. Nobby always had his own pot of marmalade when we were at college, made by an old aunt; he even took it on a rugger tour once, I remember, in Northern France. It was lethal stuff, made from Seville oranges, curaçao and triple seco, which is another orange brandy. After a night on the French beer it didn't half jerk your eyes open.

'If you go on eating breakfasts like this, Nobby, the Met'll take you off the wing and give you a decent position, like prop forward.'

He glared at me. Massenaux smiled sweetly.

'I didn't know that the Inspector was still playing?'

'Chief Inspector,' I corrected him. 'He got promoted recently. Over an affair in Brighton.'

Nobby scowled. 'I can't think why you're looking so fit and well. You've even lost weight; quite amazing.'

'Hard work. And an absolutely virtuous life.'

'Ha! Virtuous life! That's a laugh. Why—'

'Nobby,' I interrupted him, 'one of the main reasons why I invited you here, apart from my dear love of you from college days when we played rugger together, and apart from an effort to thank you, difficult though you are making it, for vouching for me to that zealous French policeman Dagallier, was for you to meet Charles. Charles, as I may have mentioned, is a star of the Impressionist department at Christerby's and an expert on bronzes. I thought, being a public-spirited sort of chap, that you two ought to meet. There are you, Nobby, chasing antique thieves and art fraud merchants all over the kingdom and there is Charles, an expert who can help you and who, in turn, would be very grateful for the odd word in his ear about this piece and that. Forgeries, for example, are your joint mutual concern; neither of you would like to be made a fool of over the occasional dodgy Corot or a Manet or so, would you? A little give and take? I know that policemen are only allowed two years or so on the Fraud Squad because temptation may eventually overtake them, but while Nobby here is on the Art section it seemed to me that a little quid pro quo might help?'

Charles took another sip of black coffee. 'With no personal interest at stake, of course? Or any benefit to White's Art Investment Fund?'

'Well, as it happens—'

Nobby banged down his cup. 'Here we go! I might have known—'

'Nobby! You are not behaving well this morning! Please confine your frustration to your subordinates, who have to listen to you. I'll order you more coffee, since you seem to have spilled most of that.' I signalled the waitress again. 'I have indicated to you both, without going into detail, the broad outline of the factory project in Carmarthen and the idea of the—Gwen Rodin, I'll call it, for short. You both now know about the fracas in Meudon. There are two aspects to this affair: one is of art authenticity, the other is straightforwardly criminal. Since you both, in rather different ways, operate internationally, there is an interest for both. For instance, Charles: can you tell us a little about the value of Rodin bronzes and the chances of one of Gwen John turning up? Or any other "work" by Rodin, representing her?'

He smoothed down his silk tie with a sigh. 'Do you want the full week's training course or the abbreviated ten-thousand-word lecture?'

'Just the simple details, Charles.'

'The value of a Rodin work depends on age, condition, authenticity, provenance, rarity. Bronzes fetch the highest prices but marble is becoming more popular than it was. Our New York office sold a small bronze recently for a hundred and fifty thousand dollars. It was a contemporary work—i.e. done in Rodin's lifetime and not a re-issue by the Rodin Museum. You see, Rodin left all his work to the State, the Rodin Museum in effect. They have the sole copyright. Only a work reproduced by the Rodin Museum counts as a genuine Rodin.'

Nobby was suddenly attentive. 'A reproduction counts as genuine? What do you mean?'

'You have to appreciate that a sculptor like Rodin could produce several editions or castings of a famous work for different clients even though they would be identical. Look at "The Thinker", for example, or "The Kiss" or "The Burghers of Calais". They are all genuine Rodins, so where do you stop? And more important, when? Take Tim's little friend Gwen John, for instance. She modelled for a monumental work to honour Whistler after he died; very appropriate also, Tim, as it happens, because she studied painting in Paris at his school and he praised her work to Augustus. But the thing never got beyond the plaster stage; it was exhibited in Paris in 1904 or thereabouts, but the International Society in England who commissioned it didn't like it and so it was never carried out in marble or bronze during his lifetime. In fact, Augustus claimed to have found the plaster neglected in an outhouse after the war. Quite recently—in 1967 or '68, I think—the Musée Rodin issued the work in bronze, a small one about twenty-odd inches high. A limited edition of twelve would be the normal thing —there's one in the Musée Rodin.'

'How much would one of those be worth?'

'Oh—now? At auction, difficult to say; forty, perhaps fifty thousand dollars.'

'This is confusing.' I ordered more coffee; that's the only problem with these Italian places; they won't bring you a pot like the English or the French. 'I can't believe that Madame Boiteau had one of those. What else did Rodin do of her? Gwen John, I mean.'

'A marble bust. That's in the Musée Rodin too. I don't like it.'

'Why not?'

He shrugged. 'Hard to explain. It's not really like her. The bronze is unmistakably her but the marble head could be anyone. Rodin had a tendency to shape the marble female heads in a certain way for a while; to me they all look the same.'

'OK. Now then, an important question: what about the possibility of fakes?'

For a moment he stared at me. Then he burst out laughing. It is a rare sight, seeing Charles Massenaux losing control to mirth; it took him a while to regain his composure, all the same.

'My dear Tim! Fake Rodins started to appear even during his lifetime! The firm that did his plaster casting was found to be one major source. Then there were all the bronze casters; Rudier is the most famous of them and highly reputable, of course, but during his own lifetime Rodin is known to have used twenty-eight different founders or foundry companies to produce his work, and maybe more. Sometimes the number made of a given piece is not known. What was to stop a crooked founder from making the odd extra one and putting it away? That would not be a fake, of course; just a stolen work. But there were fakes and there are fakes, still being made. Basically, anything not made from an original Rodin plaster is a fake. Casts unauthorized by the Musée Rodin are fakes. The work of authentication is complex and difficult in many cases. Fakers have spread rumours of a secret foundry in Normandy which Rodin is supposed to have used; pure hokum actually, but it really is difficult to separate the wheat from the chaff. You see, great work has been done in identifying all the founders' invoices but sometimes, as it turns out, what was thought to be an invoice for work done was in fact only an estimate and vice-versa. Then Rodin, like many artists, was notoriously bad about paperwork; he even left cheques uncashed for months in a pile on his desk. It's all terribly difficult. Terribly difficult.' He repeated the words with great emphasis, betraying the art auctioneer's harassment at his position, exposed by the machinations of cunning forgers, seeing himself as at once a target and a fugitive.

'So the, er, Gwen Rodin we've been offered might be a fake?'

'Of course. Actually, it would be a cunning wheeze, wouldn't it, to write to you from the Rue Babie, using an old lady for authentication purposes, to give a history to the thing?'

'While all the time some cunning French brass or bronze founder was turning out the goods.'

'Oh, it need not be French. There's a chap down in the West Country who does a very good—'

He stopped abruptly. Nobby had congealed into a sinister, threatening mass. He took out a pen and a notepad. 'That's very interesting. The West Country? Where is that, then?'

Charles Massenaux closed his eyes.

'It is your duty to report to the police any activity which—'

I should have known, I thought furiously, I should have known; the trouble with Nobby is that he takes everything so damned seriously. He won't let himself go off duty for a moment, not a bloody moment. The sight of him, notebook in hand like some smug traffic cop taking licence numbers at a red light junction, made me very cross.

'Nobby! If you don't put that blasted notepad away— now—I'll paste you one, so help me God I will! This is a private conversation!'

'You obviously don't appreciate that, as a police officer, it is my—'

'Pompous idiot! It's always the same with you! I never can get you to take off your great hobnailed boots for a moment, can I?'

He put down his implements, fists bunched, glaring at me again. 'Well, at least someone has to have a sense of what they're doing, where they're going and what's right!' His sandy hair slanted down to his reddened eyes. 'Not like some I could mention!'

'Oh? Now what the bloody hell do you mean by that?'

'I phoned your office in Park Lane the other day. They said you'd gone, off into the City trailing after Jeremy White to become a merchant wanker. Well, nature abhors a vacuum, I suppose.' He gave me a nasty, meaning sort of look, as though I should have understood.

'Eh? What on earth are you going on about? See here, Nobby, if you're going to go all bloody Delphic on me I can hardly communicate with you, now can I? Spit it out. Come on, let's have it in clear English, can we?'

He stuck his face close to mine. 'You know what I mean! You've never had the faintest idea what you were doing or where your life was leading you, have you? Or any principles worth mentioning. So you can't be surprised if you get sucked into these schemes of a City wide-boy like Jeremy

White and all this criminal violence that you attract. I'm warning you, Tim, as an old friend; you'll come to a bad end—'

'Oh my godfathers! I don't believe this! I can't be hearing right! It's Sunday School Roberts again!'

'Gentlemen, gentlemen!' Charles Massenaux interrupted sharply, leaning forward in pained reproof. 'Really! I am most sorry, really I am. This is all my fault; please accept my fullest apologies, both of you. I should have known, it was idiotic of me. I had no idea—well, I had forgotten— that the Chief Inspector would react, quite rightly, as he did. Or that you, Tim, are always quite so violent.'

Nobby switched to him, his tense expression suddenly softening. Interest flooded his face. 'Oh, you've found that, too, have you? About his being violent, I mean?'

Massenaux nodded vigorously, the creeping swine. 'Absolutely! The trade are terrified of him! Did you know that he beat up two dealers in Brighton and put them in hospital for months?'

Nobby leant back, agreement in every line of his expression. 'I should say so! I can tell you that quite apart from me—well, I've come to expect it, of course—he threatened a senior police officer in Hastings in a way that was disgraceful and deserved prosecution without—'

'—an auctioneer friend in Crewkerne thought he was going to get his jaw broken just because—'

'—put it down to his South American upbringing myself, not that—'

'Hey! Hey!' I hammered on the table with a spoon. 'That's enough! Enough! When you two have quite finished the Tim Simpson aggro memoirs, I'll recapitulate on why we're here, having breakfast on me! This conversation is getting out of hand! I've introduced you; I've advised you of a possible serious fraud from France that might involve either of you and of a very nasty gangster being in on it. I have also asked you for some information, if you would be so kind, and I've

put what I'm looking for on these notes so you won't forget.'
I handed them an envelope each. 'All right?'

It was a good job I had prepared for the meeting by
putting down what I wanted from them because at that
moment a tired-looking, overweight man in baggy grey
trousers and stained sports coat put his fat hand on our
table and leant over to speak to Nobby. His tie brushed the
surface of my coffee and I moved it in distaste; you have to
expect that sort of thing from Nobby's associates.

'We've got them, Chief! Newhaven. The dear old sailor
lads on the ferry had one of their lightning strikes just for
fun. They delayed sailing by two hours.'

Nobby gaped at him, hope flooding his face. 'All of them?'

'All of them. Squad car from Newhaven got them. Three
in the cab and the whole load, silver, everything. Pile of
phoney documents, there were.'

'Oh boy!' Nobby got up, face beaming, stuffing my envelope into his pocket. 'I'll come at once.' He turned to
Charles. 'It's been a great pleasure, Charles. I've enjoyed
meeting you, really I have. Most instructive, your information was. I'm sure we'll meet again?'

'I—er—I certainly hope so, Chief Inspector.'

Nobby gave me a sidelong look. 'As for you, you're a lost
cause. I'm going to use one of those two phrases that you
said were the only ones you needed in order to get by in a
foreign language.' He watched the waitress as she hurried
to our table with a bill. 'My friend will pay,' he quoted,
indicating me. Then he left, the ungrateful bugger, without
a word of thanks as he clapped his seedy minion on the
back.

Charles Massenaux looked at me curiously. 'My friend
will pay? What was the other one?'

'Eh?'

'The other phrase? To get by in a foreign language? My
friend will pay, and what else?'

I got my wallet out. 'Oh, er, I shouldn't bother about

that, if I were you. We were young then and you know how it is, these silly things amuse one at that age. We were touring the Paris area at the time.'

'Tim,' he said, slowly and deliberately, 'I insist that you tell me the other phrase.'

'Really?'

'Yes, really. If you want my help. The other phrase?'

I was looking at the waitress by then, poised with the completed bill. 'Please remove all your clothes,' I said.

'Nine pounds sixty pence, dear.' She didn't blink an eyelid.

CHAPTER 13

'Good morning, sir.' The old lag on the Bank's ancient lift looked at me almost hopefully, like a man touting for business. The prospect of walking up three flights, after an early start to meet Nobby and Charles Massenaux, suddenly did not attract so I got in. He looked at me humorously as he wrestled with the diagonal mesh of the inner door-cage.

'Not quite so energetic this morning, then?'

'No. I'm afraid I haven't given you much trade up to now, but I guess you get us all in the end.'

He grinned. 'I do that. Mind you, I suppose that once your Mr Jeremy takes over he'll put in an automatic and it'll be the scrap heap for me.'

'You think that Jeremy will take over?'

'Aaah—obvious, ain't it? Not immediately, like. There's one or two others in the way yet. But it'll come, won't it? After a few casualties, like.'

'I don't know. It might. From your point of view the longer it takes the better, I suppose.'

He wound a handle and the lift ground to a halt. 'Oh, I'm not worried. In fact it'd suit me to be made redundant, like.' He put a finger to his nose. 'Lump sum, they'd have to give me, wouldn't they? And I'm not too badly orf, see? Missus has got a pension as well as me, so we'd be all right, what with a little nest egg to retire with an' all. Mind you, I'm glad I didn't get invalided out after the war or retire around then.'

'Why not?'

'Well, it's obvious, ain't it? Post-war pensions was terrible, wasn't they? I stayed in till they got a lot better an' now I've got me index-linked. Just do this to keep meself occupied. But them war pensions—I mean, look at them war widows. Cryin' scandal, ain't it?'

I stared at him as he held the door open, waiting patiently but always willing to talk. 'I suppose they are. Very small, aren't they?'

He snorted. 'Pitiful. It's a national disgrace. Bloody hard-hearted the War Office always are. Expected them all to marry again, see? Well, that's not right, is it? I mean, it wouldn't suit all of them, would it, an' there was a shortage of blokes anyway. Mean, they are.'

'Must still be a struggle to cope.'

'I should say so.'

'Thanks.'

I walked down the passage to my office. In my mind's eye the little house in the Rue Babie stood neat and trim, the shutters painted. What would a girl earn, temping in Paris? To supplement a widow's pension? Were the French more generous to war widows than us? I seemed to remember De Gaulle doing something about it but I couldn't remember what.

'Tim!' Jeremy was at my desk, file in hand. 'For goodness' sake! Thank heavens you're back. Tell me all about it, at once.'

His dominant presence filled the room. Already the desk was heaped with paper and I pushed it to one side as I sat wearily down in my chair. Jeremy pulled the other chair across the little room and sat facing me as I described the meeting-place, Dechavanne, the project and Sir Richard's enthusiasm. He started braying away as soon as I paused for breath.

'Typical! He hasn't the faintest idea! Can't see where on earth it will lead us to.'

'Oh, come on, Jeremy, this is a good concept. I agree it's very far from a concept to a commercial reality, but nevertheless it is a perfectly valid scheme to look at, to consider.'

'Look at! If only he had just been looking at it there would be no problem. But he's been spending on it, tens of thousands of pounds in initial support for development work. Did he tell you that?'

'No. I must admit that he didn't. On the other hand, if you had briefed me properly I might have been expected to know. You mean he has been helping Dechavanne to fund the research on dry forming?'

'Yes, precisely. We have no business getting involved in this sort of thing, industrial investment of this speculative sort.'

'Oh, come on, Jeremy, this is supposed to be a merchant bank, founded by a merchant adventurer. Nothing venture, nothing gain. You've got to take a flyer sometimes, particularly if the concept is good and the people experienced. From my talks to Dechavanne it seemed that the engineers he's backing are sound and have been in this field for some time. I don't know for certain, of course.'

'You don't know. We don't know. It all has to do with Richard's trust, his relationship with this man. That's not the point, though. It's the change of policy, this crazy desire to get involved in—'

'Industry?' I interrupted. 'No, I suppose that's not easy for the City, is it? I mean, the City would prefer to invest in Singapore or Alaska or Timbuctoo rather than stick its money into a venture for Britain—'

'Because factories in Britain don't pay, Tim. The workers are always striking—'

'Because no one invests in bloody industry enough, so they're frightened of losing their jobs, which they have been doing, massively! If someone had been expanding our industry instead of moving everything they've got out to the States and wogland—'

'Really, Tim! I'm beginning to doubt if the City is the right place for you!'

'So am I!'

His jaw dropped. He stared at me for a moment before collecting himself. 'Good God, Tim, are you still concussed or has the sight of Talbot's tin madonna turned you barmy as well?'

I couldn't help grinning at that. It put things into perspective somehow. I rarely disagree badly with Jeremy; every now and then, of course, but not often. My reaction seemed irritable, illogical. I put my 'forehead into my hands and wiped my face, feeling the flesh wrinkle. 'I'm sorry, Jeremy. I seem to be fighting with everyone this morning; I don't know why.'

'Everyone?' His face showed a new interest. 'Who have you been fighting with already this morning, may I ask? What's her name?'

'Not a she, Jeremy. It's nothing. Just a minor disagreement with Nobby, who was getting all officious.'

'Who?'

'Nobby. Nobby Roberts. You remember him; my friend at Scotland Yard. I saw him for breakfast with Charles Massenaux of Christerby's.'

Alarm spread all over his face. 'Oh my God! This is to do with the Rodin fracas, isn't it? You're following it up like a bloody bulldog again. Tim, I warned you; you are not to get involved. Oh yes you have, though, haven't you? I can tell. There'll be a woman in it. Isn't there? Look at your face. Now look here, Tim—'

I held up a hand. 'I only wanted to alert the two of them, that's all! Doing my duty, Jeremy; it's only fair to our contacts. There's no other involvement, so calm down, my dear chap, for heaven's sake.'

'There'd better not be. Richard told me that he'd instructed you to shelve the whole thing until this Boiteau woman recovers. Which brings me back to more important matters—this mad tissue converting project. Bog-rolls and snot-wipers. Had you realized how far advanced it is?'

'No. I've just said I've no figures yet, thanks to you and Sir Richard. It's all too bloody amateur at my end.'

'Ah, well, look at this, if you want something to get your teeth into.' He produced a manila folder and handed over a sheaf of photocopied paper. There were estimates, projected cash flows, specific quotations for converting and packaging equipment, copies of applications to the Welsh Development Agency from the Banque Dechavanne, with pro-formas, organization plans and layouts. A long write-up about the project painted a rosy picture of the future. I went through them with a growing sense of alarm.

'This is all very advanced,' I said. 'I mean, it's almost cut and dried.'

'Indeed! Indeed! With so far no mention of his intention to involve White's to the very hilt and no Board authorization or even involvement. All kept absolutely under wraps. Sums advanced as investment items to the Banque Dechavanne without proper clearance, just on the Chairman's say-so.'

'Well, I suppose the Chairman is entitled to boss's privilege. He must have tremendous discretion in an outfit like this.'

'Of course, in his own field and up to a certain point he is entitled to it. What worries me—and others—is what on earth he's getting us into. Look here: the Bank does have a research department and I've been getting them to do some work, strictly on the QT for me. I have a breakdown here,

in this file, on the Banque Dechavanne. It's a very pushy,
risk-taking sort of story.'

I stifled my own fears about Sir Richard for a moment to
grin at him. 'A success story, you mean? Like Park Lane?'

He almost struck a pose. 'Tim, really! Park Lane is a
soundly-based, personal investment operation of the great-
est integrity!'

'Which means that, like the Banque Dechavanne, it has
never actually broken the law but has come as close as
possible in order to make money.'

He had the decency to look disconcerted for a moment
before smiling wrily. The pose dropped. 'Always the realist
of the operation, weren't you? I suppose that my doubts
come from the industrial nature of Dechavanne's operations.
It seems to me that there have been times, too many times,
when he has been too clever in putting projects together.
Some of them should not have come off so well. There should
have been more resistance, more competition.'

'Jealousy is a poor emotion, Jeremy. You may be good at
sound things like property, gilts, raw materials, blue-chip
shares, but there are people involved enough in certain
industries to make killings in them, just as we think we can
in art and antiques. Dechavanne is a cross between a banker
and an industrialist. It's a formidable combination.'

'Too formidable for Richard.'

I nodded. 'Now there I do agree with you. What worries
me about him is this late-flowering industrial evangelism.
It's like an atheist seeing the religious light in old age.
You are wrong in principle, Jeremy, but probably right in
practice. He's out of his depth.'

'Of course he is! Blasted river oarsman way out at sea.'

'Oh come on, Jeremy, he's been here long enough, surely,
to gain a lot of experience in some ways. He must know—'

'Been here long enough! Exactly, Tim. Precisely put.
Admirably expressed! He certainly has been here long
enough! Beautifully summed up. My uncle Richard has

been here at the Bank for all his working life. He's never worked abroad. He's been here in the City all the time. Clerical transactions, letters of credit, the London office type personified. A fort-holding operation. Richard has no experience in the field; despises it. Thinks that London is the hub of the universe and that the rest should bend to its will. He has no idea with foreigners except how to order the best claret.'

'I thought everyone at the Bank had to do a spell overseas somewhere, even if only on one of the timber plantations?'

'They have. Nearly all of them. Not Richard. He was a home-loving boy and he was good at the clerical stuff so they left him here. Apart from his house in the Dordogne and the Hundred Years' War, he's tracked steadily between Godalming and the City practically every day of his life. An interest in the Hundred Years' War doesn't exactly give you a deep understanding of modern France, now does it?'

'Well, no,' I said thoughtfully, 'not really. Although Sir Richard feels there are apt historical analogies. He is concerned, too, that the period after the loss of empire is very tricky; we might start fighting among ourselves if we don't change things. Actually he's worried that there might be another set of Wars of the Roses.'

It was a mistake. I should have kept it to myself. If ever Sir Richard's fate was sealed it was at that moment of revelation. Like a red rag to a bull, it was. Jeremy nearly burst a blood vessel.

'Oh my God! Wars of the Roses? He's absolutely barmy! We suspected it; look at the figures in those files! He's off his chump! We really feel we have to do something quickly.'

I picked up the files again. It was all very advanced and Sir Richard's annotations in the margins of various calculations gave no cause for confidence. Suddenly I looked up as the significance of Jeremy's last sentences hit me.

'We? Did you say we? We are worried?'

He looked at me, bewildered. 'What? What do you mean? Why are you staring at me like that?'

I had been peering at the photocopies before I raised my incredulous eyes to look into his, accusingly. 'You, Jeremy, are a conniving, cunning, devious, good-for-nothing so-and-so.'

'What? Have you gone mad too?'

I wagged my finger under his nose. 'These photocopies are from Sir Richard's private and confidential files. All of them. I've just realized who it is that you're going to marry that you were so reticent about. It's Mary, isn't it? The charming Mary Waller? Sir Richard's own secretary.'

He gawped at me for a moment before glancing quickly and furtively at the door to see if anyone was listening. Leaning back, he gave me a look in which admiration and guilt were equally blended.

'My dear old Tim. My dear fellow. You really do have an eye for a scenario, don't you? You really do.'

CHAPTER 14

The industrial estate at Carmarthen lies on the left-hand side of the road that leads you west towards Tenby and Pembroke. It's not a large estate and there's not much industry to speak of either. Most of the buildings are connected with agricultural activities and processes: milk, diary products, grain milling, that sort of thing. One or two firms distributing electrical gear and similar components completed the collection; it didn't take long to tour round it before I set off westwards again.

Two miles north-east of Tenby, at Gumfreston, I pulled the Volvo estate car into the side of the road, almost into the grass verge in front of the sign pointing to the church. Nearly four hours in the car and midday on the clock. My knee ached. I got out stiffly into the hot sun and smiled a grimace as my eyes took shock at the bright light outside the tinted glass. I sneezed. It was dead quiet. Across the road a farmhouse slumbered well away from the drone of a distant tractor. The grass edges were thick, full of wild weeds and flowers. No spraying of weedkillers here, no ritual grasscutting machinery milling the tops off everything. The little faded wooden sign said '12th Century Church' and nothing more.

I strolled down the ridged half-concrete trackway through the trees, winding in curves that obscured the way ahead. My knee eased up, my legs began to feel more supple. It was a magnificent South Pembrokeshire day, full of light, grass, old stone walls, buttercups and daisies. Almost at the last the track straightened out and the tree-cluttered vista opened up to take the eye across a valley to the soft rolling hills beyond. On my left, behind the churchyard wall, stood the incredible tiny old church with its tapering battlemented tower-steeple and its ancient thick buttressed walls. I opened a wicket-gate and walked down the cement path through the daisied grass around the gravestones. Half way down, on the right, set back under the trees at the edge, stood the arched grey stone and I stopped to read the inscription with my head cocked to one side to allow for the sinkage that had tilted it away from the vertical.

EDWIN WILLIAM JOHN
1847–1938
With Long Life will I satisfy
Him and Show Him my Salvation

'Ninety-one,' I said out loud. 'I won't last that long at this rate.'

Nothing stirred. It was so peaceful that I sat on a nearby mossy stone of lower proportions for five full minutes in blissful silence, staring out over the countryside, breathing in the air heavily scented by grass mowings and trees, my back to the gate.

'This is very drama-tic, boyo,' rumbled a resounding mock-Welsh voice, and I turned to watch the enormous figure of Dai Rhys Jones ambling down the cement path towards me in yachtsman's trousers, striped towelling shirt and plimsolls, with a huge grin spread all over his round brown face. Dark tousled hair topped his big head; blue eyes glinted from smooth deep slits in his well-padded features.

'Dai!'

'Tim, boy! My goodness, you've lost weight! What a surprise! I bet I could push you round easily now.' His hand grasped mine in a dry powerful grip and he thumped my shoulder affectionately, nearly knocking me over. His voice lost the mock-Welsh sing-song and went back to educated English, with just a faint trace of soft, Pembroke lilt. 'What's all this, then? By the gravestone of Edwin John? I couldn't resist it! Not any relation of Barry's is he? Fathered a rugby player or two, eh?'

I laughed and poked his well-lined ribs. 'You know very well he didn't. He sired much more passionate stuff than rugby men. He was the father of Augustus and Gwen, quite apart from Winifred and Thornton. He walked here to play the organ on Sunday every week, rain, shine or snow, for fifty years.'

He grinned. 'I know. Augustus and Gwen, is it? They used to call him Disgusting John around here. And they thought that she was a bit—funny, you know.' He gave me a sly, meaningful look. 'But it's good to see you, Tim.'

'Me too. I'm sorry to drag you away from your yacht at Milford Haven. I know that you'd rather be dodging tankers out there than be here in a graveyard but it's saved about twenty miles or more on my journey.'

His eyes crinkled. 'Don't do much dodging in the ketch. We're going for a long haul tomorrow, beating round the Lizard, so you're lucky to catch me. What's it all about?

Are we going to rob the graves or something? Have you brought a spade?'

Perhaps, I thought to myself, I'm picking up Sir Richard's sense of history or, at least, his version of it, but I kept that to myself. It's odd how certain themes, once started, persist. 'No, Dai. I thought this would be a good spot to meet you because although I've booked us a table for lunch at the Imperial in Tenby, overlooking the beach, the walls have ears. Especially in small Welsh towns.'

'Welsh? Welsh? Call me a Pembrokeshire pig if you like, but never call me Welsh.' He chuckled richly at the old saying.

'Well, whatever you all are around here now—daffies or something like that. How's the paper merchanting business going? Still very prosperous?'

'Can't complain. Not going into it, though, are you?'

'Let us say that someone was trying to persuade me to. Not paper merchanting, actually, but tissue converting, even tissue production. Soft absorbent tissue, that is, not the shiny stuff you pack your dress shirt in.'

His eyes widened. 'What, a mill? Like the one at Bridgend?' He seemed quite horrified. 'I suppose, well, I suppose if you can have one in South Wales you can have another, but—'

'Well, forget production then. Just converting.'

'Converting? Making bog rolls, you mean?' He grinned broadly. 'That's a soccer player's business, Tim, not a rugger man's.'

'What do you mean?'

'English football player, Frannie Lee, remember him? He's got a factory doing it, north of Manchester. Very successful, I believe.'

'I remember him, all right. Scored a winner against Wales once; I saw it on the telly.'

'That's right. A Welshman never forgets a defeat or an insult, you know.'

'Who does?'

He gave me a reproachful look. 'Come on, now, Tim. Allow us a little Welsh character part now and again, there's a good fellow. You English hog everything.'

'Character part! When you were right prop forward you used to try and shove the opposition right round so I'd get the blame for letting the scrum go skew.'

'Kept you on your toes, didn't it? Stopped you from getting lazy.'

I smiled at him. His bulk filled the churchyard-field with robust life, broad and cheerful, dispelling the past like bright sunlight.

'It's in Carmarthen. The proposed site of the factory. I looked at it on my way through. There's a small industrial estate there, mainly agricultural products, dairy stuff, milling, you know. An odd place to choose. You're practically a local man, Dai. Do you have any contacts in the Welsh Development Agency?'

'The WDA? One or two, why?'

'Would they really give grants towards a factory there?'

He threw his hands up in the air. 'Ho! They'd give grants if you'd put up a factory anywhere! Desperate, they are. It's like Northern Ireland on another scale. It's not their money anyway, is it? It comes from the EEC Regional Development Fund. It's Mickey Mouse money, Tim boy. To create employment. To give away, in other words. You can't keep up with it; they open up and shut down faster than you can count.'

'Are there a lot of rackets?'

His eyes went sly again. 'Of course there are. When Government interferes in business the rackets multiply, don't they?'

'What sort of rackets?'

He shrugged. 'I'm not a business criminal, Tim.' His eye caught mine and he grinned. 'Don't look at me like that. Just an honest paper merchant, that's me.'

'So how's it done?'

He giggled. 'Now that's not fair. Actually, I'm not in that sort of thing, so I really don't know the clever ones but, for instance, over-invoicing must be one. The WDA give a one-third grant towards equipment, say. So if it's foreign equipment you get the supplier to over-invoice, pay him out with your money and your one-third grant and then collect the over-invoiced part back off him again. In Switzerland or wherever you want it.'

'Well, well. That's a thought. Dai, if I asked you, could you get me a quotation for some converting equipment? Pretend that you're thinking of expanding into the converting business?'

He looked dubious. 'I don't do much tissue, Tim.'

'Only a container a week, imported from Portugal through a nominee so you don't upset your other clients.'

He did a double-take. 'How did you know that?' His voice was indignant.

'Just let's say it's a small world. You could get your nominee to inquire. It's nearly all Italian equipment and some German packaging gear. A very big lunch, it will be. I'll give you all the machine references and model numbers. Done?'

He laughed suddenly. 'It's a deal. If you tell me how you found out about my container.'

'I've got news for you, Dai. It's not Portuguese.'

'What?'

'It's Brazilian. Same language. Your man in Lisbon trans-ships it; he's a merchant, like you.'

'Well I'll be damned! He told me that it was from a local mill supported by the government. The lousy so-and-so. Here, for that I'll give you a bonus. You're interested in Augustus and Gwen John. Come on; I'll lead the way into Tenby and after we've had lunch I'll show you something.'

He walked back up the path with me and heaved himself into a new Aston Martin at the top. After all, he'd said that trade was not too bad. I had trouble keeping up with him. Turning off by the great fortified town wall of Tenby, he passed the tennis courts and then pulled up outside the Imperial, well ahead of me. In the bar, as he downed a pint with gusto, we chatted amiably about old friends, long-forgotten matches and the current lamentable state of the game of rugby.

'Dreadful,' he said sadly, accepting another pint. 'Hardly worth leaving Swansea to watch a game these days.' He caught my eye and giggled again. 'I know; I haven't missed a match in ten years.'

'It's the beer that keeps you going to them and you know it. That and the bit about being able to say, "I was there."'

He looked moodily out of the window without replying, along the South Beach to Giltar Point and Caldy Island, across the sparkling sea. I knew what he was thinking; there's no compensation for not playing any more, not being in the thick of it, hearing the roar of the crowd instead of being part of it. Life's later defeats and victories have none of the sharpness, the clear-cut emotions of youth's sporting triumphs and disasters.

'Come on, Dai,' I said, 'we'd better eat. I have to drive afterwards.'

I had insisted on a table at the window, with its spectacular view. The sun was so strong that we needed a blind to shade our eyes as we ordered; the Imperial is one of those old-fashioned resort hotels where the menu includes five courses and shirking is disapproved of. Dai cheered up again as the waiter noted it all down.

'Dai,' I said eventually, 'you used to work in a real paper mill, didn't you? Before you took to making money as a merchant and importer. Producing real paper, I mean, in a British mill. What do you know about dry forming?'

He pointed out over the receding tide on the magnificent beach, past the castle on St Catherine's Rock, eastward across the broad waters, the channelled sea, the distant lumps of land rearing above the horizon in random bergs of grey matter.

'Bristol,' he said, with a grimace as he chomped down a quantity of egg mayonnaise. 'Bristol. That's where you should have gone, a few years back. Not now, of course; be wasting your time, now.'

'Why?'

'Why? Because St Anne's Board Mills has gone now, Tim, like many other great British paper and board mills. Shut. Caput. Finished. I got out ahead of time. Five effing great paper machines they had—ever seen a paper machine?'

'Yes.'

'Well, there you are, then. Looks like an ocean liner the first time you see one, doesn't it? At least, like the engine-room of one. All those huge drying drums, in banks. Well, you could have nipped down the side of Temple Meads station and helped yourself. St Anne's Board Mills was one of the prides of Bristol. Belonged to a tobacco company; much easier to grow and sell tobacco, isn't it? In plantations.'

'That has a familiar ring. It was a conventional mill, though, wasn't it? You mentioned all those drying drums.'

He let the waiter take our empty plates and put down the soup before replying. 'They had a dry-forming project. Not for tissues; theirs was for board. It was an arrangement with the Dane, Karl Kroyer. The doyen of dry-forming processes. They never got to commercially successful production because the mill went under in the Great British Paper Mill Collapse of '81 and '82. High pulp costs. High energy costs. No lame ducks, no Government help. Phut. Ellesmere Port, St Anne's, headline stuff; plenty of others just slipped quietly under.'

'So it wasn't really the dry forming that wasn't viable? It was the whole business, for everyone?'

He blew on his soup before slurping it off the spoon with a yachtsman's lack of concern for decorum. 'Development costs and experiments. It's a bottomless pit, Tim. You should know that. And, in that business, a patent agent's pet minefield. The Americans with Kroyer licences spent time suing each other for triple damages, three hundred and fifty million dollars, cheerful sums like that. Not to mention the rest. It's a big league, for big boys. Even the Yanks and the Scandinavians have had some spectacular collapses and they're sitting right on the raw material. As to the French, they're no different: government bale-outs, workers' sit-ins, you name it, they've had the lot.'

'What about the small-scale idea?'

'Small is Beautiful, you mean?' He sighed. 'All I can say is that up to now it hasn't been. Maybe it will be. Maybe. New technology may make white elephants out of existing mills. Maybe. I don't know. It hasn't happened yet. You can't point to a success story, so that means you're a pioneer if you get involved. And you know what they say about those.'

'Never be a pioneer.'

'Correct. The beef looks terrific.'

'The original White was a pioneer. Up your Amazon. He made a lot of money.'

Dai practically spat. 'Plantations. Raw materials. Buying and selling. Timber. Like tobacco.'

'You're in a very negative mood, Dai. Nothing venture?'

'You tell me; you're the City gent. Is paper a good business?'

'I have to admit that the return has been diabolically low.'

'So there you are! This is excellent beef. Why are you bothering?'

'Because converting is quite different from basic production, as well you know. It's very hard to tell, but my guess is that there are some people doing very nicely out of it, thank you. Customers of yours, some of them, riding round in Rollers.'

He put down his knife and fork for a moment as a slow grin came to his face. 'Funny you should say that. I must admit I've been tempted to put in a machine or two myself from time to time.'

That's the most infuriating thing about talking to people in business; they never give you anything like the true story, not if they want to make any money themselves. I wagged a finger at him. 'So who'll be the Franny Lee of South Wales? You?'

He laughed. 'I'll stick to merchanting, like a good rugger man. That sweet trolley looks tremendously attractive, doesn't it? I wouldn't normally but we'll be on ship's biscuit for days after tomorrow.'

'Some chance.'

When we had finished coffee and he watched me pay the bill with great satisfaction he gestured at me affectionately. I followed him out of the hotel and on to the promenade that overlooks the South Beach as far as the rocky headland at Giltar Point. For a large man he moved quickly, almost nimbly, striding along until we turned right, away from the magnificent view, into Victoria Street.

'See that house there, called the Victoria Hotel? With the yellow door and windows?'

I nodded. It was a tall narrow Victorian terrace house with three bay windows, one on top of the other, set in a stuccoed façade. Above the parapet two tiny dormer windows stuck out of the sloping roof. He gesticulated towards it.

'They came from Haverfordwest really, but that's where they lived when the mother died.'

'Gave her a taste for attics,' I said, thoughtfully.

'Eh?'

'You see those two dormers, right in the roof, at the top? Well, that's where the children's rooms were. Much of her time in France she lived in dormered attics like that. Not at the end, but a lot of her rooms were up at the top of a house. The paintings show them.'

'Really?'

'Yes. Perhaps she felt safe up there, away from the ex-
posure of the big rooms. She spent a lot of time trying to
get away from him, of course.'

'Who? Her father?'

'Yes, her father, but Augustus too.'

'Why, Tim?'

'He was disruptive; he bullied her when they were small;
he created massively tense emotional situations like his
ménage with Ida and Dorelia; he was like a great centrifugal
force hurling everything outwards, Bohemian, drinking,
whoring, talking, performing—yes, that's the word I was
looking for, he was like a one-man circus performance—the
great ham artist with a girl on each arm. She was the exact
opposite. Odd, really, that she ran away from the presence
of Augustus straight into the arms of a somewhat similar
man, because she couldn't work when he was around,
either.'

'Who's that?'

'Another Augustus. Name of Rodin. Thanks for the tour,
though, Dai. I must leave you to your ketch. Be hearing
from you? Soon as possible?'

'You bet.' He smiled fondly at me. 'You haven't changed,
Tim. Still got a head full of odd historical and biographical
facts, you have. An intellectual magpie, as I always used to
say—ouch! You lousy English bugger, I'll get you for that!'

CHAPTER 15

When the sun shines on the City of London the stockbrokers,
bankers and general all-round gamesters in charge of things
usually make for one of the social events of the summer
season. It's hard for regular working people to grasp, but a
gambler does not have to hold to ordinary fixed routines.

He keeps going until he has made all the money that game or session will allow, or his luck changes and then he relaxes. Nine o'clock in the morning and five in the afternoon have nothing to do with it. Sometimes the sessions are long and involve waiting for foreign sessions to start or finish; sometimes the games are short but at unsociable hours. Behind him and supporting him the clerical workforce provides the gambler with systematic fixed-hours services; banks have to open and close at regular intervals, books have to be balanced, accounts kept, computers programmed. The gambler himself has different deadlines to keep.

Sir Richard White and Jeremy were both dressed for Ascot. Both were in a filthy temper. Sir Richard was in a filthy temper because he was being pressurized by Jeremy to disgorge the figures Jeremy already had and he was being kept from proceeding to Ascot. Jeremy was in a filthy temper because Sir Richard was being recalcitrant and he, Jeremy, was also being kept late for Ascot. Outside the Bank Sir Richard's Rolls waited patiently; Jeremy's Jaguar stood behind it. In the office anteroom Mary Waller sat modestly, eyes lowered except for a brief flash at Jeremy and a quick smile at me as we had passed on our way in. It seemed to me that we were on rather a sticky wicket. We couldn't admit that we had got the figures without provoking a major explosion and the certain sacking of Mary Waller, which would rather spoil future family relationships, if they mattered. If we said that we were suspicious of the figures, Sir Richard would demand to know on what grounds and what figures; even the very fact that we were picking on this project and forcing an emergency meeting was, in itself, fraught with danger. Jeremy had called what amounted to a crisis meeting with his uncle because, following my visit to Carmarthen and chat to Dai, he got into a great temper about the whole idea of the project. Jeremy's instincts were turning out to be City instincts after all; there was a feel to a set of figures, a smell to a story that those instincts accepted or rejected. Somehow, something was amiss. On his own, Jeremy would have simply said, 'Don't confuse me with the facts, I've got decisions to make.' Hamstrung by his uncle, he was having to go through an exasperating charade in order to nobble the project. The line that he had been taking with his uncle hadn't helped. It was rather like Matron with a doubtful sufferer: take this medicine, it's very nasty but it will do you good.

Tim Simpson was, of course, the nasty medicine. If he had had any doubts about the flavour before, Sir Richard appeared to be quite convinced now. He glared at me from time to time as Jeremy insisted that his uncle cough up the files on the Dechavanne project. The fact that we already had them and the liaison with Mary Waller were both undisclosed to the luckless Sir Richard, still unaware of the treachery around him. He was thundering back at this frontal attack upon his fortifications.

'You ask me to meet you here today on an urgent matter! I find that it is not only not urgent but that it involves a direct slur on my judgement by you, a junior director who has hardly even started his career here! New to the Board!' His eyes swivelled round to me again. 'I suppose this is at your instigation? You dare, without full information, to question my assessment, inexperienced as you are?'

'How can he form any judgement of the matter without the figures?' Jeremy was hot with indignation. 'You agreed to bring Tim in on this. You can't half-do it. It is perfectly normal procedure and you know it; this Frog might be taking us for a complete ride.'

Sir Richard's well-clad figure stiffened. 'I have known M. Dechavanne for several years. He is one of France's most successful younger bankers. There is no question of his risking his reputation on some—some—'

'Speculative project?' I said helpfully, drawing his ferocious glare. 'The fact is, Sir Richard, that I think I have said once before, in Brazil perhaps, there is an optimum size for any business and it's always much bigger than you think. This project has the stamp of a classic pattern on it; the conventional converting project, way out in Wales, which may or may not be successful but which you will have to keep going willy-nilly, perhaps throwing good money after bad because you'll be waiting for, and funding, the dry-forming research in France which justifies the whole project. Who'll own the patents, if any are granted? How far have you agreed to go? Where does the commitment end?'

'That is a matter which I shall have agreed with Henry Dechavanne.'

'On your own?'

He paused for a moment, looking at me with the disbelieving gaze of a man unused to impudent or challenging questions from subordinates. For just that pause an uncertainty crossed his face. Then his jaw opened and snapped shut with a final grimace.

'I will not be subjected to this—this—browbeating by junior directors and members of staff,' he snarled thickly. 'I am leaving. Now.'

'You won't give us the files?' Jeremy demanded incredulously.

'No.'

There was a silence. The Chairman of White's Bank started to gather things up from his desk, preparing to leave.

'Sir Richard,' I said, in a last desperate attempt, 'I am very sympathetic to this type of project in principle. It is just the sort of thing that I like and would love to commit the Bank to joining. But the checks and balances one uses in banking have to be applied just as much in this as in—'

'Indeed. And I shall apply them. Without interference from Jeremy. Or you.' The obstinate set of his features was final. He picked up a pair of gloves from his useless blotter. You bone-headed proud old bugger, I thought furiously, there's no dealing with you, is there?

At that moment he embodied, for me, all the old, stuffy, privileged, inside-circle aspects of the City that I most hated and despised; the sort of insulated I've-got-it-and-I'm-hanging-on-to-it exclusiveness that made my hackles rise like porcupine quills. Why did I feel different about Jeremy, I wondered, and caught momentarily at the answer: he was of a welcoming disposition, indeed he positively burgeoned under the influence of new talent around him, taking delight in the spread of it. Sir Richard was the old type, careful to preserve people in their place, unexplaining, keeping them confined to the order of things in nineteenth-century fashion. Yet Sir Richard wanted to expand into modern Anglo-French technical cooperation; Jeremy instinctively wanted nothing to do with it. They were precise opposites of each other, with contrasting qualities at either end of a personal and business scale. It was a paradox.

At that moment, however, it was Sir Richard's obstinately superior exclusion that maddened me most. I decided to put my oar in, to use an apt phrase, and see if I could make Sir Richard catch a crab or whatever it is that oarsmen do when they get in a mess. I cleared my throat.

'The commitment to the converting project itself is very substantial, Sir Richard. The equipment alone will cost three million four hundred thousand pounds.'

He looked at me, startled, putting down the gloves. 'How do you know that? You're guessing. Where did you get such figures from?'

I ignored the swift look of alarm on Jeremy's face. 'From the Welsh Development Authority, in Cardiff.'

'What? You—you went to the Welsh Development Authority? Without my authorization? You asked for such figures? They gave you the figures? You mean you made us look like fools? Do you have no sense of loyalty or discretion?'

'Oh yes I have, Sir Richard.' I looked square into his livid face as I lied. 'After I'd been to Carmarthen I called to discuss the chances of the success of our application with the WDA officials responsible. It's perfectly normal. I pretended during the discussions that I'd left my detailed factsheet with the equipment information behind, here in London. Since we are supposed to be co-partners with the Banque Dechavanne the official obligingly reminded me of the amount on the application and showed me the pro-formas. Very friendly people. Only too glad to assist, particularly when I pretended that we were considering a larger investment.'

He gaped at me in bewilderment. A look of stifled amusement and gratitude crossed Jeremy's face as he visibly showed relief. That'll teach you, I thought; next time I talk about preparing for meetings properly you'll listen, maybe. Maybe.

'Well, you see, Sir Richard,' I went on, 'I had to follow up all our own very interesting discussions, so I went to Carmarthen myself to get the local facts, the full picture. I'm afraid that's my training; always reconnoitre thoroughly. I must say I find Carmarthen a bit far from any chimney-pots.'

His exasperation would have been funny if I hadn't been so close to him. 'What on earth do you mean? For God's sake speak English, man. Chimney-pots?'

'Oh, sorry. A bit far from centres of population. For a consumer product that's bulky and light, like converted tissue, it seems a long way away.'

'This must stop at once! I will not have you running around the countryside without my authority, like some sort of boy scout. This is a confidential project and I will decide what programme of work will be carried out. You will not take any action until you have precise instructions from me. Is that clear? You might very well have prejudiced an important aspect of the project, quite apart from making us all look fools in the eyes of the Welsh authorities.'

'In that case, Sir Richard, would you please let me have

access to the files and the facts available to date, so that I can understand matters fully?'

He drew back his lips from his teeth in a grimace of fury. 'No! I will be the judge of what work you will do on this. When I wish you to carry out work I will tell you.'

'May I ask, in that case, what was the purpose of my visit to St Emilion?'

'To report to me. On your ridiculous failure over the Rodin piece. And to be given background information on this project in what I hoped was a memorable and enjoyable fashion in case you were to be needed at a future date. I see now that your sense of self-importance excludes treatment of that sort.'

Poor old Sir Richard; he was trapped. I could see now that, somehow at Jeremy's instigation, he had half-started a ferret in hopes of keeping things under control and now regarded it as having bitten him ungratefully. A ferret had not been what he had really intended to accept in order to allay Jeremy's fears; a Dalmatian would have been preferable to Sir Richard; a spotted dog to run behind his carriage.

'Sir Richard, I regret that there has been a misinterpretation, on both sides perhaps, of the role I was to have played in this project. Perhaps it would be better if I withdrew from the whole thing altogether.'

'Certainly not! I will not waste time in briefing further assistance! You will make yourself available to me, as I agreed with Jeremy, as and when I require it.'

'No.' Suddenly I'd had enough of him, the whole thing, the lot.

'I beg your pardon?'

'I'm afraid it won't do, Sir Richard. It seems, as I have said, that there has been a misunderstanding on both sides of the role I should play. I am not prepared to join your gang of tame ferrets nor to be Jeremy's pet dog. Unless I have a clear understanding of what professional role I am to play I shall not be able to continue.'

His jaw dropped. I don't suppose anyone had cheeked him very much before and survived. His nostrils flared. Somehow, somewhere, there had to be an aspect of his behaviour that would explain his extraordinary secretiveness, his concealment of knowledge and his obstinate desire to play half of a game with me. He was keeping control of himself but only just, and almost sneered as he spoke.

'Jeremy was anxious to have you join us. Against my better judgement I agreed. As far as I am concerned, my reservations have been amply justified. My use for you is in a subordinate role as assistant in such tasks as I define. I did not expect you to go rooting about like a Jack Russell and I certainly would not have had you prying into matters which I had not authorized. I must now agree that neither I nor the Bank require the services of an insubordinate, conceited egoist.'

My first reaction was to hit him, but he was old. My second was to resign, quit, forget the whole stupid idea then and there. But of course you never do that. Quite apart from it being a luxury few can afford, all upbringing restrains it. Besides, you quit when you choose the timing or you make them fire you, but you never resign. I opened my mouth but I reckoned without Jeremy, who had been uncharacteristically quiet. He had already moved closer to his uncle, half-blocking him from me. His voice was low, missing its usual ebullience, deadly serious.

'Richard, this is unacceptable. The matter is my responsibility, not Tim's. It is quite clear to me now that you agreed to let him join you on this project in some sort of hope that he could be kept out of his depth or neutralized in useless errands until it suited you. I now even doubt the existence of the Rodin thing at all; it could easily have been a clever red herring on your part. You should have known better. Unless you impart the information needed to assess the tissue project properly I shall have to raise the whole issue at the next Board meeting in two weeks' time.'

His uncle picked up his gloves. 'If you wish to make a fool of yourself and damage your career here, that is your affair.' He looked across at me with cold contempt. 'It's a pity you couldn't find a more suitable cause.'

Clutching the gloves, he marched abruptly across the room and out, wrenching the door open and leaving it swinging to reveal Mary Waller's white face. Jeremy and I stared at each other blankly over the void left by his departure.

'We forgot to give him a tip for the two-thirty,' I said.

'Tim! Don't be flippant, damn it! This is serious! I shall have to use those figures.'

'You can't. You can't put Mary into that position. And it's all too soon; you're rushing your fences.'

'Nonsense! I—oh, hullo, Mary.'

She had come into the room tentatively, with a very harassed expression on her pale face. Jeremy put his arm around her shoulders once, and embraced her before letting go. She looked at me searchingly with a countenance that needed reassurance.

'Tim, this is awful. I know what you must think, but it's not so. I would never normally have let Jeremy get into Sir Richard's files even though you know how close we are, now. I had to make an exception of this; it's alarming. All his old caution and judgement seem to have vanished. The Bank's been doing so badly; I just couldn't help telling Jeremy. I'm really terribly grateful to you, Tim; I heard you lying about those figures you said you got from Cardiff; but it will take much more to deal with this.'

Jeremy put an affectionate arm around her shoulders again. 'My dear Mary, stop tormenting yourself. Of course you did the right thing, but I shouldn't have put you in this position even though it was bound to come sooner or later. Now we'll just have to deal with it sooner than we thought. Tim protected you well, like a good fellow. I'm quite confident.'

I shook my head. 'It's too soon, Jeremy. The other members of the Board'll not back you, yet, in a leadership contest. Don't make Old Talbot's mistake; you're trying to charge the cannon park before the main force has come up yet. You'll get massacred.'

'Tim, what on earth are you alluding to?' He shook his head with a grin. 'You do talk in riddles sometimes.'

'Sorry. But I meant it. You'll have to use those figures plus a great deal more to dislodge Sir Richard. Or uncover something totally out of order. Actually, you see, your uncle's got the right idea in many ways but his execution of it is lousy and clouded by some sort of mad idealism. And you, well, you, Jeremy, are opposed to the whole thing blindly, in principle. So I'm not sure which of you is the worst. I feel caught between two stools. Perhaps it would be better if I ducked out anyway. Sir Richard will have his knife out for me with a vengeance from now on.'

'Oh no!' Mary Waller stepped across and put her hand on my arm. 'Please, Tim. Jeremy and I have such hopes; we've talked and planned so much about the future, and you've always been in our plans. Please.'

'It would be silly to bugger up Jeremy's strategies for the sake of my situation. Jeremy is not just a member of the family, he's *the* member of the family for the future. If this Bank is to be preserved he has to play his hand correctly. That means choosing his battleground carefully. This is too soon and too small an issue; the other directors won't support Jeremy for the sake of a new and tetchy member of staff who's cheeked the Chairman over a tentative project in Wales. There has to be a tangible case of some sort. Be realistic; it won't stick. Besides, it's not important, I—'

'No! It is important!'

'Look, Mary, the Chairman of a private Bank is perfectly entitled to play things close to his chest. Do you think that a Dechavanne tells his co-directors half of what he's really at? I bet he doesn't.'

Jeremy intervened with stately confidence. 'Richard's judgement must be checked. This is the City of London. There are rules on disclosures and all companies of any sort have regulations concerning capital commitments and the flow of information to Board members.'

'Which are there, like all rules, to be avoided. Every head of every company has his own slush fund; it's the normal thing.'

'Well, it's too big, in this case.' Jeremy was resolute. 'I told you, Tim, that we—and I meant we—are going to knock the stuffing clean out of this Bank, and we will. Actually, I'm grateful to you for bringing the whole thing to a head so soon, even though I do believe that you must learn patience, dear boy. In two weeks' time I am going to march into that Board meeting fully armed and you are going to be the one who provides the missiles. You remember what I said about the old Tim Simpson who up-ended Park Lane years back? And Brazil? Well come on, Tim, you've got the files and you've got two weeks. It should be a doddle for you. You're frightfully good at this sort of thing, you know you are. So that's the strategy; Ascot, here I come.'

He took Mary's arm and they walked back to her ante-room, leaving pug-ugly number one alone with his thoughts.

CHAPTER 16

The commissionaire at Christerby's actually nodded as I walked in through the double doors. It gave me a pleasurable frisson, in a way. From time to time I had bought some pretty expensive articles in those rooms, on behalf of the Art Fund, but I imagined that compared with the sort of heavy buyers and dealers that crowd those rooms every week my contribution had been hardly noticeable. Familiarity with the building enabled me to make my way up to Charles

Massenaux's office, a windowed cubbyhole in a frowst of similar cubbyholes on the second floor. Around its walls were bookshelves, bursting with the same reference books and old auction catalogues that I had in mine. Behind a plain oak desk sat Charles, in an imitation-leather swivel chair, listening to the telephone with a scowl on his face. He waved me to the other chair in the room and I sat down. When he had finished his call he replaced the receiver and looked at me without lessening the scowl in any way. He placed his hands on the desk top and peered at me, his long face severe.

'There are things,' he said darkly, 'that are better not said on the telephone, one finds. So I hoped it was not too much of an imposition for you to join me here. I realize, now that you are no longer in the West End, that you have to trek out from the City, but I thought that it might be a pleasure for you. After all, the City is such a cultureless place. It surprised me a bit, I must say, to hear of your move there. In some ways I've often thought that you might be better placed with us or one of our fellow-competitors, in the rooms here in the West End. More your style, I would have said.'

'I couldn't live on the salary,' I retorted. 'To work for you lot one has to have a private income; auctioneers are notoriously low payers. And since you're not allowed to deal on your own account—or at least you're not supposed to although I guess you can use nominees—it makes things unattractive. Can't see how you pay all those school fees otherwise.'

His scowl deepened, condensing his long face. 'Don't push me too far, young Simpson. You've done enough damage to me today as it is.'

'Me? What have I done?'

He pressed his hands down harder on the desk top. 'Not you perhaps, but that Robert of yours.'

'Eh?'

'Robert. Bobbie. Peeler. Cop. The fuzz, the filth, the pigs, whatever your local terminology may be. The appropriately-named Chief Inspector Roberts.' His mouth drew into a line.

'What's Nobby done?'

'Only gone and arrested poor old Ivor Lieberman, that's all. Locked him up, he has. Disgraceful, I call it.'

'Who's Ivor Lieberman?'

'A founder. Brass and bronze. In Taunton, or near it, at a village nearby.'

'Oh dear. Was he—?'

'Yes he was!'

'I'm afraid Nobby's a bit zealous at times, as you may have gathered. What did he nab this Leiberman for?'

'Forging bronzes. Barye bronzes, to be precise. Horse sculptures, nicely signed, very popular they are.'

'How did he—Nobby, I mean—get him?'

'Red-handed, by all accounts. It's a bloody shame. Poor old Ivor has been making animalier bronzes for years. Everyone knew that. Well, nearly everyone. Grudging him a living is a mean trick.'

'Charles, are you, of all people, defending a known forger of extremely expensive Barye bronzes?'

'Of course I am!' He put his face nearer to mine, to lend emphasis to his words. 'One of the lessons you have yet to learn, my dear young Tim, is that the inner circle of the art world is very small indeed. We all have to make a living and there's no point in adopting a dog-eat-dog attitude. One of the great things about having dear old Ivor around was that I could always recognize his work. Forgers are artists, just like the originals; they have their own little quirks and eccentricities. So whenever a particularly expensive-looking animalier turned up I could always tell if it was one of his. Hello, I'd be able to say, here's one of old Ivor's. If it wasn't, then I'd have to start taking it seriously. You see what I mean; only the foreigners or some greedy ignorant punter with more money than sense would buy Ivor's work on spec, hoping for a bargain. We always knew.'

' "We" is you and the boys of the inner circle, eh, just like the City?'

'Exactly.'

'Anything for the quiet life, the predictable scene?'

'Absolutely.'

'And what about the poor devil who got landed with a forgery and lost all his money?'

'Pooh! If he's in the Trade he should know better. If he isn't then serve him right for buying without an expert opinion.'

'Like, say, yours?'

'Of course!'

'That is the most morally reprehensible thing you've told me for years. Almost as bad as the financial attitude of the City. Tell me, just as a matter of interest, did Dear Old Ivor ever turn his hand to Rodins?'

'Oh yes, often.' He shook his head sadly. 'He was never any good at Rodins, I don't know why. But he did some really smashing animals. Cracking good stuff. We used to recommend anyone who brought one to us to put them in a provincial auction.'

'Nice of you. Not a dog-eat-dog business, you said.'

He ignored my sarcasm. 'Well, anyway, he's behind bars now and that means I'll have to look out for a newcomer. A gap like that is always filled by someone. It was the Russians last time; bronzes of lesbians, would you believe?'

'I'd believe anything of you lot and the Russians, now.'

He pulled open a drawer in his shabby desk and pulled out a small bronze of two unclothed ladies writhing in what I took to be a form of ecstatic embrace.

'Two thousand of those,' he said, smacking the thing down on the desk-top, 'were shipped out of Russia about two years ago. All over Europe. Look at the bloody thing; it's well made, you know. They fetched anything from forty quid up to three hundred, depending on how gullible or lewd the buyer was. I know, it's not really art forgery of the kind we've been talking about but it just goes to show. Incidentally it was your query about Rodin that reminded me of this little number; he was a bit keen on depicting that sort of thing, too.'

'Disgraceful. Is that what you wanted to tell me?'

'What? Oh no, sorry, this business of Ivor has quite put me off my stroke. It was the French gentleman friend of yours. I contacted our Paris office for you.'

'Thanks, Charles.'

He held up a hand. 'It will cost you, young Tim.' He grinned. 'Actually, there's not much to it; he is a very keen collector, but not, apparently so far, of Rodins or of sculpture. He's a porcelain man.'

'Ah yes, I know that—'

'Wait for it, young Tim, wait for it! Let Charles tip you a wink. The really keen interest of your Monsieur Dechavanne's life, the thing on which he is known to be a ruthless, cunning, really unpleasant collector is—guess what?'

It dawned on me as he was saying it, so that I held my finger up to point at him.

'Don't tell me, let me guess! It's Sèvres, isn't it?'

He clapped his hands. 'Bravo! Ten out of ten! You're absolutely right! He is the most notorious collector of Sèvres in our Paris rooms. Now there's a connection for you! Isn't there?'

CHAPTER 17

I came out of Christerby's and walked to Piccadilly with my hands stuck in my pockets, slowly ruminating. By instinct I ambled as far as Green Park and then hopped on a bus to

Victoria. The pub where I had arranged to meet Nobby was a good five minutes' walk further on and he was already at the rail, mug in hand, when I arrived. It was one of those modern mock-Victorian pubs with red flock wallpaper, red carpets, thickly-glazed brown woodwork, brass light-fittings and mirrors with mock-genteel beer ads on them that say 'cordials and mineral waters purveyed to the gentry' or some such crap. Mock pub tables with iron bases stood beside more red plush on the seats and benches. I gazed at Nobby in horror.

'Do the Yard know that you drink in a place like this?' I demanded.

'Of course,' he said blandly, with a quick glance around. 'No self-respecting criminal would be seen dead here. I can relax, well, almost relax, anyway.'

'I ought to kick you,' I said, 'but you can stand me a pint instead.'

He grinned. 'Been to see Charles Massenaux, have you? I like him; that was a good intro for me, Tim. Bitter for my friend here, please. A pint, and two ploughman's. We'll be over at that table. Come on, Tim. Cheer up: you look half-baked today.'

'With people like you destroying all my carefully-built relationships, it's hardly surprising.'

'Nonsense.' He was in a cheerful, confident mood. 'Charles was very grateful to me. In return for pinching Ivor Lieberman I tipped him off about an extremely nasty collection of paintings in a private house sale; one of his assistants could have made a very embarrassing mistake.'

'Oh.' Trust Charles not to have told me the other part of the story. 'I'm glad that you and he have become such chums.'

'Now then, now then; no unpleasantness, please. Remember that you started all this for your own mendacious ends. Which reminds me: I've got a bit of paper for you.'

'Oh. That's better. What's on it?'

He shook his head and flashed a glance at me. 'I shall give it to you and you will put it away quietly in your pocket and we will not discuss it. Walls have ears. Actually there's nothing exciting in it, really. Your friend has no form; he's a rough, ruthless type, but then aren't all up-and-coming businessmen the same? The computer saved a lot of time, personal details, father, mother, that sort of thing. Used to take a lot of tracking down. Now that we're all on record, it's no—'

'All? On record?'

'Yes, all. You, me, everyone. The French are particularly keen on computerized data. Your friend Dagallier seems a decent sort of Frog. Mind you, I wouldn't push a French cop the way you have the British; no sense of humour like us. Remember that time in Lille, after the match?'

'Oh yeah?' I put away the folded sheet of paper he gave me carefully, in my inside pocket. 'Your sense of humour wasn't very evident the other day. Taking your job very seriously, you were.'

'Ah well, I was a bit edgy perhaps, I agree. That was an important pinch for me. Did I upset you? I thought it was rather a good breakfast; didn't spoil it for Timmy-boy, did I?'

Only three days ago, I thought, and his version was already quite different from mine. What was it that Wellington had said? The history of a battle is like the history of a ball; everyone who attended will have a different version of it. Nobby was today the lean, muscular cheerful man I had known so well at college, the swift wing-threequarter of zest and invention, not the sour, tense policeman of the breakfast. His quick eye sparkled at me from under the sandy thatch of his hair as he looked pointedly at his empty glass. I got two refills and sat down again.

'How's Gillian?'

He polished off the rest of his cheese and pickle, speaking

with his mouth full. 'Fine. Great. We were talking about you, last night. She sends her best.'

'Thanks. What were you criticizing this time?'

He shook his head. 'Nothing. Except, well, except that she said it's been a long time since Carol.'

'My divorce was three years ago. So?'

'Well, I must say that women do have a point, you know, Tim. Especially when I look at you.'

'Eh?'

'Now don't get all violent. I mean, since you got divorced you've been roaming about, all kinds of scrapes, hopping in and out of bed with God knows who—'

'Jealous?'

'No. No, I'm not. But Gillian did ask me to ask you if you've seen anything more of that nice girl, the one that went to Australia, Sue Westerman, now we both liked her. Gillian thought that you might, well, you know—'

'No, I haven't.' I tried to keep my voice natural.

'Pity. Pity, that. I mean, it was quite obvious, wasn't it, that she really didn't want to go, but there you were, like a bear with a sore head, tantrums all the time, little legs drumming on the floor—'

'Hey! Hey! What do you mean, she didn't want to go? She was mad keen to go. She couldn't leave fast enough. There was no stopping her. Her career came first, it was the Great Opportunity and all that. How do you think I felt?'

He blinked at me over his glass. 'Oh, come on, Tim, you can't rationalize it that way, now, surely? Not even you. I mean, it was bloody obvious; the right words from you, or actions I should say, and she'd have dropped the whole thing. But there you are, I suppose, that's life. You weren't ready for it and she had her pride, after all. I mean, you've always been a bit offhand with the girls, do you remember that one in Girton you—'

'Stop! Stop right there! Now let's get this clear: Sue Westerman was adamant about that job in Australia. I begged her not to go but she said she had to, it was a unique opportunity in her career. It's over ten years since we left college, you know, Nobby; girls nowadays expect to live a full life, become Prime Minister, Chairperson of ICI and Vickers, it's not the old fireside slippers and the Little Woman any more.'

He drew one corner of his mouth sideways in a disbelieving grimace. 'It never has been for some, Tim, and I guess the some are becoming more numerous. But that's not the point; you never did anything to stop her.'

'She couldn't be stopped!'

He shook his head. 'There were things you could have done to stop her but you didn't. You just went on living in your old scruffy bachelor dump and doing your job and treating her as a pleasant appendage to your life. She was bound to bring things to a head. It was clear to all of us; your friends, I mean. She obviously didn't want to go but you forced it.'

'My God! Talk about different versions of history. So now there's your version of what happened and mine, and Sue's, and doubtless Geoffrey Price will have a version, and Jeremy, and Christ knows who else and they'll all be different.'

'No.' He grinned wickedly. 'Just yours and everyone else's.'

'Bastard!' I laughed at him, though, because his well-meaning humour was difficult to resist. I suppose the reason why I have kept in touch with Nobby, quite apart from our youth together and his usefulness as a member of the Art Fraud Squad, is that although he sees life from a viewpoint that is a bit stuffy and moralistic, he is, basically, sympathetic to most human beings. It may seem a contradiction that, but a lot of people with a strong social purpose lack both humour and sympathy. Nobby was not like them.

He shoved off back to Scotland Yard with a cheery wave. In one respect I felt I had made an important change from the description he had given and that was in relinquishing what he called my 'bachelor dump'. I had moved into Onslow Gardens to a flat that was much lighter and airier, with a rather nice flowered wallpaper. I even bought a new settee, a large one, and some other furniture. But the rest of what he said baffled me. It was becoming like a conspiracy; I recalled Sue saying 'you could have stopped me if you wanted to' the night of the burglary. Collectively they were shifting the blame, or some sort of blame, on to me; I scowled as I caught a taxi to the Bank.

Jeremy had left our research department's file on the Banque Dechavanne on my desk and I took out Nobby's paper, unfolding it and smoothing it as I added it to the documents. As he had said, there was nothing terribly exciting in it and Dechavanne had no criminal 'form'. His was a conventional background, his father a reasonably competent middle-class accountant, his mother—well, at his mother I stopped short.

'Anglaise,' I said softly, staring at the paper until the phone rang, breaking my trance. 'How very appropriate.'

'Pardon? Hello? Is that you, Tim?' The voice had a quiet Pembroke accent.

'Dai?'

'Yes, it's me, Tim-boy. What's appropriate?'

'Oh, nothing, Dai. Nice to hear from you. What's up?'

'Nothing's up, Tim. I've got that information you asked for, from Italy.'

'What already? How?'

He chuckled, a deep chuckle from the end of a long line. 'I can see that your Bank is going to have to learn about modern communications. I got it telexed, you chump.'

'Of course. Of course. Did they give you the exact details?'

'Oh yes. Got a quill pen and an inkpot handy, have you? Seated comfortably on your high chair? Here you go: one slitter-rewinder model—'

I started scrawling rapidly as he listed the different pieces of equipment, the reference numbers and types. Core winders, log saws, embossing units, packaging machines, wrappers, conveyors and other ancillary units completed the list.

'Quite a grand total,' he said, when he had finished. 'That should keep you busy for a bit. Minimum export prices, those are, and no messing. My man has dealt with them before, so there wouldn't be any messing, see?'

'Perfect. Just perfect, Dai. May you always have jolly old boating weather.'

'It's been a pleasure, Tim, as they used to say the morning after. Keep your head out of the ruck now, won't you?'

'No fear, Dai. Cheers.'

'Cheers.'

Another click, into place. I picked up the research department's files again. There were details of the Banque Dechavanne's capital funding and its involvement in various projects. A tissue mill in or near Victoriaville caught my eye; where the hell is Victoriaville I wondered, it sounds colonial, Australian possibly. No; my atlas said Canada, Quebec to be precise. So he had got experience, at least you could say that for him, and of course it would be in a French-speaking area. Impressive, really; North American tissue production experience, even in Quebec, was not to be sneezed at. I put the file down. Two days gone already. Two days since the great fight with Sir Richard. Twelve more left to prove that he was either rowing along with his back to a forthcoming weir or that he was involved in something we didn't understand. I closed the file with a snap. I was going to have to go back to France again. It was quite clear that I should have to present myself back under Dechavanne's nose and pretend that I was still Sir Richard's squeaker for the project. Only that way would I get the full presentation, the insight to the process and the doubtless bodged-up figures given to impress visitors from potential sources of finance. Before that there would be time to check Dai's figures against the stolen ones from Sir Richard's cabinet, the private one. There was also a little checking to be done in Paris first, but my sequence was working itself out very satisfactorily in my mind, so I felt quite confident. It all goes to show you; as flies to wanton boys . . .

About lunch-time the following day I got a taxi outside the Bank and told the driver to take me to Millbank, to the Tate. The restaurant was full and the buffet fairly crowded, but I found her, in the corner, with a sandwich and coffee, talking to another girl.

'Tim! What are you doing here?'

The girlfriend excused herself tactfully and left. I sat down facing Sue. The brown hair, soft and full, framed the clear-skinned face and humorous eyes, which looked quizzically at me in surprise. She was wearing a striped blouse or shirt tucked into a neat skirt and therefore looked, as usual, competent and smart, in control of herself and her life.

'I'm on my way to Paris,' I said irrelevantly, disconcerted by the sight of her.

'Via the Tate Gallery? I didn't know that the Cromwell Road went past here.'

She was mocking me. I scowled as I replied. 'It's not so far out of the way and there was something I wanted to ask you.'

'Ah.' She nodded in comprehension. 'I see. Not a Godwin sideboard this time, or a painter called Mary Godwin either, I suppose? It will be about Gwen John or Rodin, will it not?'

'No.'

'Oh, you've read those notes I gave you then, have you? And what further assistance do you need?'

'I—er—I've read them, thanks, yes. Very useful.' I lie badly.

'What then? Some new investment problem? What is it this time?'

'For heaven's sake, Sue, will you let me get a word in edgeways?'

She raised her eyebrows in reproof as she lifted her coffee cup and gestured, still mocking a bit, for me to take the floor. Her face had changed to a more interested expression.

'What the bloody hell did you mean when you said that I could have stopped you from going to Australia?'

The coffee cup stopped half way to her lips. Around us the clatter of cups and saucers, plates and knives, seemed loud as June tourists, talking a load of cock about Art, came off the queue at the self-service counter and rattled themselves to tables, speaking loudly. She blinked at me and put the cup down, carefully.

'Tim, I'm not—I'm really not strong enough to start a row with you all over again. Really I'm not. I have to give a lecture in—'

'I'm not here to row. I just want to know. You said that if I'd wanted to I could have stopped you from going. So did Nobby. I don't understand, you see. I thought I had pleaded—'

'Nobby? Nobby Roberts? When did he say that?'

'Oh, the other day, it's not important, but I—'

'Not important? You and Nobby Roberts were talking about me? About us? Really? How was that? Who brought it up?'

'I—well—it—' The thought dawned on me, quickly, that love is a game of the type that a Dechavanne would play well, in which truth is less important than the objective. If I said that Nobby had brought it up, had instigated it, her reaction would be quite different to the news that it was at my initiative; her view of my interest would be quite different. 'Er, I asked him,' I said, taking on an earnest, sincere sort of look, quite successfully for once. 'It seemed to me that I ought to, well, after what you'd said, to find out what he really thought because he and Gillian, you know, they know us both well and it was a second opinion from a friend.'

I put on another earnestly-seeking-after-knowledge expression that might have been quite convincing.

'You asked Nobby if he thought that I would have stayed?'

'Yes. I mean, I'm sorry if that upsets you but I was confused. After what you'd said.'

'What did Nobby say?' She leant forward, her coffee forgotten. 'Exactly, now. Tell me exactly what he said. He must have been very surprised at the question. Give me his exact words.'

Just like a bloody schoolmistress, you see she is. Come on, class of little boys, tell teacher exactly what the answer should be and don't fluff your lines.

'Well, he was—er, yes—he was a bit taken aback. He hedged about a bit at first. A friend's feelings at stake, I suppose.'

'And then?'

'Well, then he said that, er, you were right. He said that he and Gillian thought you would have stayed. If I had, um, well, you know.'

'What?' She was looking at me really intently now, totally absorbed.

I shrugged slightly. 'Well, if I'd, obviously, done something that I didn't do, you know.'

'Such as?' Mischief had come into her face.

'Well, that's it, really, you see, that's what I've never understood. I mean, I thought that you were happy with the situation. You—you never wanted to marry or anything drastic like that, you said very definitely, or at least not then. And I thought—'

'What?'

'Well, you were always keen on your career and you wanted, I don't know, some sort of independence, so—'

'So you let things be.'

'Yes. Yes, I see now I, um, perhaps I did just sort of carry on, you know, a bit perhaps . . .' I let my voice trail off uncertainly.

'Perhaps what?' Teacher-types are remorseless.

'Thoughtlessly, I suppose.'

There was a pause. She tapped her coffee spoon against the side of her cup. She wasn't looking at me when she spoke. 'You were awful when I said I wanted to go to Australia. Awful. You behaved dreadfully.'

'I was hurt.'

'Just like a child. You never really inquired into my side of it at all. Just tantrums and don't go.'

Incredible. Absolutely incredible. Women can make themselves believe in the rationality of their most absurd actions. I bit my lip.

'I was upset. Tired and emotional.'

'Oh yes, drunk. Often. You never thought to change anything about your life, to see what it was I wanted. Tell me, Tim, where were you when I came back from Australia? You never bothered, of course, to find out exactly when I'd be back, did you?'

'I, er, I had to go to Chester.'

'Had to?'

'I tried to phone you. It was an emergency. I tried all week. You were avoiding me.'

'You didn't think of actually finding me, seeing me, did you, until you got back to Town?'

'It was a genuine emergency, Sue.'

'And I wasn't. I'd keep until you got back. Who was talking about their job coming first?'

'Touché. Well, it doesn't now.'

'What do you mean?'

'I think I'll have to resign. I'm staying to finish, or try to finish, a job before the end of next week. Then I think I'll have to go; I've said unforgivable things to Sir Richard White and you can't cheek the Chairman and expect to get away with it.'

'Go? Leave Jeremy? What does he say about it?'

'Oh, he says, you know, stay. To be honest, I'm not sure what to do.'

'Tim, you *are* getting into another crazy scrape, aren't you? I can feel it. When is your flight to Paris?'

'Oh, soon. It doesn't matter. There are lots of flights to Paris; it's not important.'

She gaped at me in surprise. 'Are you all right? This isn't like you at all. You were always so conscious of time. I—' Suddenly she looked at her watch. 'Time! My God! I've got a lecture hall waiting for me! Oh, Tim! I'm sorry but I have to dash. Really I do; I'm sorry, I can't leave a lecture hall full of people, I'm giving the Renoir lecture today. I have to go. Oh Lord! I have to go.'

'Of course you have.' I smiled a bitter-sweet smile, just managing to hold back the obvious comment about jobs coming first but seeing her, flustered and upset, realizing that she had become a victim of deadlines. 'I'll see you when I get back.'

'All right. All right. No, listen—don't go to Paris. No, there's no telling you, is there?' Agitated, she picked up her satchel-handbag and made off, glancing back as she practically ran from the buffet towards the stairs to the ground floor. She called back once, though: 'See you soon, Tim?' and was gone.

'If Arthur will allow it,' I murmured to myself, as I threaded my way out after her, slowly.

CHAPTER 18

The flight to Paris got me in during the late afternoon and I trailed to my hotel off the Avenue Wagram without hurry. The weather was hot and the traffic frenetically circling the Arc de Triomphe raised dust and fumes around its glitter. It was too early to eat so I strolled out of the hotel, bought a paper and wandered a short way down one of the neighbouring avenues—the Hoche, I think it was—until I found a café-terrace and ordered a beer while I idly leafed the paper, not really seeing its pages. If ever a man was in a state of flux, I was.

Whether or not I cleared up the tissue project for Jeremy, it seemed to me that I had to clear my mind about my work at the Bank; that was if Sir Richard had not already pre-empted any decisions on my part anyway. It's not often, I thought, that a man can have his job and his romantic life so well thrust into the melting-pot simultaneously. Sir Richard was to the Bank what Arthur was to Sue; symbol of my own apparent choices and actions. I could simply have obeyed Sir Richard; I could have taken more notice of Sue. But it was too late in both cases; after all, if you wanted to select a more directly opposed person to the sort of man I was you couldn't do better than Arthur. A gentleman, Sue had said, which apparently meant someone who has no physical appetites or at least never expresses them; a museum curator without commercial desires or involvements; patient, willing to wait; almost everything that you could think of that would cancel out me and my type. Change is inevitable, I murmured. The only thing I was now sure of, after a morning of study, was my ability to pin down Dechavanne over his project. Of that I was, sitting there on the Avenue Hoche, pretty confident. As I have said, it all goes to show you; as flies to wanton boys . . .

I glanced up over the unsighted pages of the newspaper to look through the café window up the avenue. There were a lot of cars parked under the broad, leafy pavement expanses on either side of the road, ranged as they often are along the wide Parisian boulevards in glittering ranks. Behind the shade-dappled vehicles across the road, in the deep shadows of the sheltered side under the big grey classical buildings, a few people walked and the occasional pedestrian was checked by the offers of the odd tart plying her trade among the passers-by. Paris in the late afternoon and early evening, I thought, with a wry smile; adultery time. One of them, half-hidden in a doorway, had a white blouse and a cotton skirt, with an expensive leather handbag on a smart strap over her shoulder. She was plumpish and dark, so that the impression I got was of a girl rather like Jacky Boiteau. I finished my beer and rummaged for some francs to pay the bill; I decided I would go back to my hotel and have a shower before going out to eat. As I glanced up again, across the street, a man stopped by the girl in the far doorway and she leant forward to speak to him. Her face was much clearer out of the dark door-shadow and I saw her quite distinctly. It was Jacky Boiteau.

There had to be some mistake. It couldn't be. It was. She was waiting for a boyfriend then, or a man friend because this man seemed older than—no, she was talking to him, watching him and, finally nodding as she stepped out of the doorway. I sat, rigid with horror and disbelief. He didn't take her arm or anything friendly or affectionate like that. He just walked close beside her, quickly, looking neither left nor right but dead ahead, avoiding other people and slightly behind her, so that she could lead the way. Exactly as a prostitute does when she has agreed a price with a man for the services required and is leading him to the hired room where they will be carried out.

At that very moment Auguste Rodin and I had a sort of experience in common. His father had a first wife who died, leaving a daughter called Clothilde. She was, obviously, half-sister to the younger Auguste. It was she who defended his early drawings and insisted that the dull, backward boy be sent to school. Eventually she strayed from the path of virtue and was banned from the family. One day the grown-up Rodin was swaggering through the brothel quarter with some male friends when, with a glad shout, his half-sister ran out of a doorway to greet him. I don't know how it felt to Rodin, and Jacky wasn't my half-sister, nor would she be glad to see me, but my stomach felt as if someone had kicked it.

There are two reactions you can have in that situation; you can freeze, helpless, collapsing into tearful despair, or you can move like a mad bull in a red rage. I was across the street regardless of traffic and sense, at a run, and closing on the pair before I was even conscious of it. As they turned into a side street studded with small hotels I caught up with them and gave a shout. The man turned, nervously; he was slight, shabby, unremarkable. She glanced back with composure and curiosity at first, then stopped, her face congealing in shock.

'Hop it!' I snapped at the bloke. 'Go on! There's been a mistake, an error. The girl is with me.'

I've never seen anyone scarper so fast. He scuttled off down the street so quickly that I found myself staring at Jacky, alone, wondering whether it really had happened at all. I grabbed her arm and drew back to the corner of the avenue, my teeth clenched.

'What the hell—' I began to snarl, but had to stop. Blocking the way was a thick individual, bulky, full of menace. Oiled hair capped a squat head. His lightweight suit was cut wide, double-breasted, loose-trousered. The tie he wore was too bright and his gut was too big. His face scowled.

'What's up?' he demanded, jerking his head at Jacky.

Her reply was unprintable. Even the pimp paled slightly but his lips drew into a mean smile.

'You will have to pay,' he said to her, incomprehensibly. 'Both for this one and for the one who has gone.'

Horrible intelligence dawned. I turned to Jacky, my nostrils flaring in disgust. 'Is this your pimp? Is that what he is?'

'No!' Anger and tears filled her face. 'He has nothing to do with me! He is always trying. I do not know him. Believe me, Tim, please!'

'Shove off, Alphonse.' I put my hand on his chest and pushed him back, out of the way.

'He's got a knife!' Jacky screamed at me, terror contorting her face.

I just had time to let go of her and turn back as I saw him dip his hand into the wide-boy's jacket, which was a bloody silly thing for him to do. It left him with only one arm free for that quick, split-second moment that his other hand was inside the broad lapels. I hit him, unobstructed, right in the middle of the face, practically on the point of the nose. Caught off balance, he staggered back a pace and I kicked him hard on the kneecap, still boiling with rage and hatred and the desire to kill something. With a shriek he lurched forward, the leg giving way and the hand with the knife now in it sweeping uselessly down towards the point of agony. Checking himself, he managed to make a half-lunge with the knife towards me but he was like a spider with one leg gone, crippled, slow, and I bashed him again, on the side of the jaw this time so that his head went over and he fell sideways, hitting one of the peeling plane trees on the pavement as he stumbled.

'Tim!'

Getting out of a big Citroën next to the tree was another thug, half way out already, radiating violence. Jacky's warning shout gave me just enough time. There was sufficient space and clearance between me and the car to take two battering-ram strides and slam the opening door, trapping him half way out. He managed to stop the scissor-action between door and sill from snapping his shinbone but he was pinned, writhing to pull out a weapon, one arm inside, one out. His face was above the door, hissing at me. Using my left to keep him trapped, with my weight against him, I swung a right and hit his head. It bounced on the metal car roof like a punchbag, and came upright. He tried to hit me with his free arm. Teeth clenched, I hit the head again, bouncing it on the roof. And again. And again. And again, until it stopped bouncing. I let the door open and he slid out on to the ground, blood seeping from his nostrils. It's a bad sign, that, especially as I hadn't actually hit him on the nose. I grabbed Jacky again and ran her, squealing, across the road, towards the Arc de Triomphe and then down the inner side ring road to the Avenue Wagram.

'Tim! No! You're hurting!'

'Run! Run, you stupid bitch, before the police get here!'

Through the lobby door into the hotel reception I kept a grip on her, although she wasn't really resisting. The key-porter opened his mouth, looked at me, closed the mouth and handed the key over, turning quickly back to some imaginary business. I ran her up the stairs, not waiting for the lift and practically flung her into my room.

'What do you think—?' she began resentfully, but I stopped her.

'Sit down! Sit down there, on that chair!'

She did as she was told, shivering still with shock and fear. 'You have no right, what are you doing, following me?'

Rage and fury seethed in me. I could cheerfully have hit her. It's the last time, I thought bitterly, the last time anyone plants a girl on me again or I ever believe in spontaneous physical attraction like the mug I've been.

'Shut up! Who are you working for? Sir Richard? You'd better tell me!'

She stared at me dumbly. 'Working for?'

'Yes, working for! I should have realized, shouldn't I, that evening you came straight to my door here in the hotel. You didn't send a message from reception like any normal girl would; you came straight up. I was tired and sleepy. They know you, don't they, on the reception desk? Like a lot of the hotels round here, I suppose. They're quite understanding about that sort of thing. You have to pay the porter a douceur of course, or that pimp of yours does, or whatever the arrangement is. So tell me now quickly what's the clever deal? The whole Gwen John thing, it's a put-up job, isn't it?'

'Gwen John?' Her jaw dropped. She looked as though she

had taken a blow to the back of her head, sandbagged. Slowly, her chin drooped and she brought up her hands to either side of her face to support it. It was a position of utter despair and I suddenly felt quite sorry for her. After all, she was probably being used as a small pawn for practically nothing by way of reward in someone else's game.

'You better have a drink.' A bit ashamed, I went over to the mini-bar and got out a cognac. Business entertainment, I thought bitterly.

'It was the only way I could thank you.' Her voice was muffled. 'I thought you liked me.'

'Here, take this. Go on. Thank me? For what?'

She took the glass, sipped a little, coughed, and looked up at me, numb and perplexed. 'My—my aunt. And me. The attack at our house. You're the first person I've met for ages who made me feel that there are still some men about who would protect a woman, treat her with kindness and courtesy; a gentleman, in fact. I thought you were so nice. You were so embarrassed when you had to leave because of your boss's telephone call, so charming and upset about it. Most of them—' she tossed her head towards the window overlooking the street—'can't wait to get out afterwards.'

She began to cry. I got myself a Scotch, dreadful doubts beginning to dawn. The sight from the café had triggered off a whole red-rimmed angry sequence of thought that might be completely wrong. I sat down on a spare chair, facing her.

'Jacky,' I said, gently now, 'why did you pick up that man? Why were you standing there, like a tart? You are a tart, aren't you?'

She bit her lip. Then she finished the cognac before she looked at me defensively, resentment tingeing her expression. 'How did you think it was possible to make ends meet, there in Meudon? Eh? On my aunt's pension? And she can't draw it while she's in hospital. The bills keep coming in; I used all the money we had.'

'Your aunt knows that you—that you—'

'Of course not! My aunt means everything to me. She sacrificed everything for me.'

'But where does she think that the money comes from?'

'From my job, of course! With the agency here, in Paris.'

'While all the time you've earned it from—from the streets?'

She glared at me, angry now. 'Not all the time! I've tried! I've really tried. You think that there has been a bad time only in England? I can't make ends meet from temping. Every good job has dozens of applicants. Everything is so expensive. Especially in Meudon. I couldn't ask her to leave Meudon; it was her home, her life. All her memories. So, once in a while, when the agency had no work for me, when I had to have some cash, I—well, I'm ashamed that you know it, but I had to. She never knew; my aunt never knew.'

'She just saw you going off to work, to the train, and coming home again in the evening?'

'Yes.'

There was a silence. I found that I had skinned my knuckles somewhere during the fracas and I blew on them. Bugger history, I thought, what about young, unhappy, near-to things; and battles, here and now. Once again I'd put my foot right in it where a woman was concerned. She sat in hopeless misery in front of me, like the born victim of a struggle I would never have wished to see.

'There's nothing for me!' she blurted out suddenly, resentful. 'Nothing! There's no Rodin thing, nothing. My poor aunt must have been deluded. Or it's gone already and she didn't know it; perhaps it's been stolen. I've searched all over again, everywhere. Nothing! It's hopeless. She'll probably have to stay at home, bedridden. How will we manage? How?'

There was no answer to that. I still had to get some very

unpleasant thoughts off my chest. 'The—er—thugs, just now. Pimps. Don't they control, I mean, aren't they—'

She shook her head vigorously. 'No. I refuse to have anything to do with them. Of course, when there is trouble, like when you interfered, they try to move in. They say they give protection, they threaten, demand money. But I did not work regularly so I avoided them.'

'Dangerous business.'

'Yes.'

I didn't know what to do, then. I was out of my depth. I wished I'd never seen the Rue Babie, made such a bright suggestion to Sir Richard, visited the aunt in person instead of waiting for photographs, documentary evidence. But the Chairman of White's Bank had been adamant: get over there, get on with it, don't wait about. Almost obsessive. Could Sir Richard have set me up? Surely not; but here I was, in addition to the whole Gwen/Rodin drama, the tissue project, everything, up to my neck in another drama, tragic this one, involving me. I should have listened to Jeremy; don't get involved, he'd said.

A peremptory knock on the door resolved any question about what to do next.

'Police! Open up.'

Oh well, I thought, here we go, this should have Sir Richard and Jeremy all agog once again. Street fighting with pimps this time. There was nothing I could do so I opened, standing back quickly and submissively in case a tough gendarme should think he might have to subdue the inmates. Just as well; a large uniformed man, tense with muscular alertness, came in first, followed by another, very watchful plain-clothes man. After him, cigarette, dark jacket and all, came my old mate Dagallier. He gave a start of surprise and astonishment, not at me but at Jacky.

'Mlle Boiteau! Oh! Excuse me. This is most unfortunate; I thought you were at the hospital.'

She shook her head, lowering her eyes. I remembered

something I had once seen in an old movie about the French police registering all women in prostitution and a pang of dismay went through me. Dagallier collected himself.

'You have not heard the news?'

She shook her head again, suddenly looking up anxiously at him.

'I am deeply sorry, Mlle Boiteau, to be the one to convey bad news. Your aunt died this afternoon at the hospital, without recovering from her coma. Please accept my deepest sympathies.' He glanced round quickly at me. 'The situation has now changed, of course. We are now treating this case as murder.'

She sat stunned. I put my hand to my face and wiped it, pressing the fingers round my forehead and over the eyelids with despair. Everything was out of hand, everything. Jacky began to cry again, tears running large down her face. A penetrating moan came out of her. The uniformed heavy looked totally confused and the plain-clothes man stared at Dagallier, disconcerted. I put my arm around Jacky in a hopeless attempt at comforting her. It was Dagallier who assumed control of the situation.

'You will need to go to the hospital,' he said briskly. 'Mlle Boiteau, this gendarme will take you, now, to the hospital where I regret that formalities will have to be completed. It is better that this is done as quickly as possible and I ask for your collaboration, with all due sympathy of course, in getting it over with. Please go with this officer, who will make all the necessary arrangements and who will look after you.'

'I'm very sorry about your aunt, Jacky,' I said, feeling useless. 'It's terrible news, but he's right. The sooner you get it over with, the better.'

She nodded dumbly, still hardly in control, and left with the uniformed man. Dagallier closed the door and came back in, lighting a new cigarette. He looked at the other plain clothes man and then shook his head sadly at me.

'More of the *galanterie*, eh, my dear Mr Tim Simpson? Not an appropriate moment, I'm afraid.'

'How on earth did you find me here?'

'Oh, I am a policeman, remember? But it was not so very difficult, after all. When I got the news of Madame Boiteau's death I telephoned your office to tell you and presto! They said you were here. So, after finishing some work I decided to combine a visit to Paris on other matters with the opportunity of seeing you here and what do I find? I find myself converging on the hotel with other policemen; I find, in the foyer, a colleague from the Vice Squad of this *arrondissement* who is chasing a man and a woman after a fraças in the Avenue Hoche and who have been seen running into this hotel. I find that the porter confirms the arrival in a—dishevelled—state of the couple in question and, *extraordinaire*, who should it be but you? Of the woman I had no knowledge. *Incroyable*, but that is life in the police. So, I insist on accompanying my colleagues up here, luckily for you. They thought that you were very dangerous and involved in a vice ring struggle for power. The two men you, er, disabled are well known and considered to be very nasty but not that tough physically. Their aptitude is with a knife. Not, for instance, in the same league as your friend Falco.'

'The Vice Squad?' I sat down heavily. 'I only, er, well, you know—'

'Went to the assistance of a lady?' Dagallier smiled crookedly. 'Who was attacking her this time?'

His colleague watched me without expression. I decided to keep it straight. 'No one. It was all a mistake. Mistaken identity, I expect. They attacked me in error.'

Dagallier raised his eyebrows. 'A mistake? You arranged to meet Mlle Boiteau here, or nearby? And then you were attacked?'

I thought of Jacky's expression, her fear at the entry of the police, the old movie. 'I—er, yes, I—'

Dagallier frowned. 'Let my colleague advise you of the

notes he has made. From eyewitness accounts. Then I think
you should give us your answer. Thinking carefully.' He
turned to his partner. 'Please.'

The other man cleared his throat. 'I don't need my
notebook. The woman Boiteau was standing in a doorway
touting for business, which is an offence. She and a customer
were walking away when they were intercepted by a man
—you—and the customer departed. The two men then tried
to impose themselves; they are well known to us, I can give
you their names from memory. It was not difficult to follow
your progress here. Credit us with some intelligence, Mr
Simpson. As for the woman, Boiteau, if I were to make
inquiries at local cafés and bars I should doubtless obtain
confirmation that this is not the first time she has been seen
in the area. And in its hotels.'

'I see. I'm afraid it was a shock to me. I guess you've
pretty well got everything.' I confirmed my role in the
incident to them quickly. 'What will you do now?'

The Vice Squad man frowned. 'I'm not sure. The woman
Boiteau has broken the law, technically, and should be
recorded by the incident. You have obviously not been
involved in any criminal way, except in this breach of the
peace. Inspector?'

Dagallier took the cigarette out of his mouth. 'You have no
further news about this Rodin piece? She told you nothing?
An extraordinary coincidence, your meeting, you must agree.'

'Nothing. I've made inquiries in London but there's nothing so far. I planned to go to the Rodin Museum tomorrow.
Otherwise nothing. I hoped perhaps you—'

He shook his head. 'Nothing has been found here either.
And Falco has disappeared. For the moment.'

'If this is now a murder inquiry it makes Jacky—er, Mlle
Boiteau—and me your major witnesses.'

'Correct.'

'It's no problem for me but she's a sitting duck. In
Meudon, I mean.'

'True. And do not be so sure about yourself, especially while you are in France. Or even in London. It has now become a matter of great urgency to find Falco.'

'What about Jacky Boiteau?'

'I shall put a guard on her house, temporarily.'

'Good. But I mean this business here, in the Avenue Hoche. It was awful.'

He looked grave. 'This has been a very sad affair. I think that once the formalities have been completed the best thing she can do is to leave both Meudon and Paris. She will presumably have inherited the house and this may give her a chance to start a new life elsewhere. Who knows? I am a policeman, not a keeper of people's morals.' He looked at the Vice Squad man. 'Anything more? No? In that case we will leave you. With a warning.' At the door he paused, waiting until the other man had gone. 'Your friend Inspector Roberts; he made some inquiries about a certain banker, here in France.'

'Oh, did he?'

'Come now. You are also a banker; you are a friend of Inspector Roberts: did it have anything to do with this affair?'

'Not really.'

'Not really? What kind of answer is that? I hope you are going to be absolutely frank with me. I am a policeman and I hate mysteries.'

'I assure you I will be. If I have any concrete facts you will have them, I promise you.

'Very well.' He held up a warning finger. 'And, really, no more *galanterie*, eh? Not just for a while. You have used up all your credit.' He gave me a quick wink, then he was gone.

CHAPTER 19

The Hôtel Biron in Paris was once the town house of a johnny-cum-lately, early eighteenth-century version. Then it belonged to the Duchesse de Maine, who was a daughter-in-law of Louis XIV. After that it went through a series of flamboyant roles until its owner was guillotined in 1793. Successively it was then a kind of Vauxhall Gardens; the Russian Embassy; a convent and, by 1905, an empty shell used for artists' studios and evening orgies. Yes, real orgies. Rodin moved into a bit of it during 1908 and it is now the official Musée Rodin, completely taken over by his work. Write me a cohesive history of all that, with its obvious lessons, if you can.

Near to the Biron's long-windowed yellow façade the finialled dome of the Invalides glinted in the hot sun. I had spent the morning elsewhere in Paris digging up no new information and I regretted the wasted four or five hours. It was a relief to look at the symmetrical block, the long, stylish windows, the pedimented centre section. Inside, the cool marble hall, full of sculpted figures, calmed the irritated seething in my mind. I decided to take it easy, get into the subject a bit, not knowing what I might find. It was all famous stuff, nearly all of it, anyway, and it was sobering to stroll round and see so much impressive sculpture. Not that I understand the medium well, especially the impressionistic approach of the later work. It was upstairs, in Room 14, that I found the little bronze figure of Gwen John posing for Whistler's Muse and I stopped before the undraped figure on the plinth which put the face at the same level as my own. It was her all right, with sloping chin and open mouth, stooped in the position for which she posed for so long, the left knee up, armless, sad. Learned writers have traced Rodin's classical source for the pose back to that of Melpomene, of the Louvre Museum Sarcophagus from the mid-second century AD. I had thought that, for the Whistler monument, Gwen John was originally conceived as holding a pencil and sketch-pad in her hands, but since there were no arms it wasn't something I'd bet on. It didn't tally with the description in Fritsch's book either, but since that had gone in my burglary I couldn't check. Frustrated, I stared at the bronze long and hard before moving to the marble bust.

I had to agree with Charles Massenaux. I didn't like the marble bust, but then I don't pretend to have understood it. To me it fell into that category which Charles had mentioned, in which all the women's portrait busts had a sort of pneumatic tyre of hair swathed round their heads and were somehow all similar. I wouldn't have known that it was Gwen John at all if I hadn't deliberately asked an attendant. Thinking about it, I wandered into the next room looking at a bust of Clemenceau and then others, when I thought I saw a portrait of Augustus John in oils hanging on the wall. It wasn't; when I got closer I found that it was Rodin's father, painted by Laurens in 1860, the beard and black flowing hair having deceived me at a distance. And yet, and yet; it was a strange irony that Gwen should flee from her brother into another, similar fold.

Someone with time could spend months of their life reading Gwen John's letters to Rodin, two thousand of them, preserved at the Hôtel Biron. Not me; eleven days were left, that was all, and my quest was not to be pursued the way of academic research. I took another turn round the museum and its grounds. Somewhere in a shed here, after the second war, Augustus John claimed that he found the plaster statue of Whistler's Muse, the one exhibited in 1905, neglected and forgotten. I wondered what had happened to the plaster sent to England and rejected, according to John, by the Society of Painters, Sculptors and Engravers 'on the advice of Derwent Wood because of an unfinished arm'. Did he mean that it was armless? Fritsch says that it was not the statue holding a medallion of the painter but a smaller one and that it never came back. But then Fritsch, writing in 1939, could have been wrong; his description of the design of the monument—'Whistler in a Roman toga, surrounded by three or four muses, of which several busts survive—' does not correspond with modern accounts of the work. I was starting to confuse myself again, or history was.

I was surprised to see the bronze of Gwen John undraped. In my mind's eye I could see a photograph of the plaster muse, the legs draped with material, to emphasize the hips and the raised knee which, unclothed, rose clear of the more complex mass of material and rock. In the reproduced bronze she is completely nude. So which was the genuine Rodin? One, the other, or both? I shrugged as I left; many paintings exist in several original versions so why not a piece of sculpture? Gwen John herself had the habit of tracing the same drawing several times and then colouring each version differently to try several effects of tone. Perhaps her '*maître*' had done the same.

I felt tired when I got back to the Avenue Wagram. My work for the day was finished but my mind was far from easy. Out in Meudon, my conscience kept saying, poor Jacky is alone, mourning her aunt's death. She will be sitting in the house in the Rue Babie, guarded by a policeman, utterly isolated, with no one to comfort her. Surely not, a counter-conscience said, some neighbour will be in, advised by the police, they always do that, get a woman bobby— do the French have police-women? they must—to sit with her. For a while, anyway. It's not your business, it's a family matter, don't for God's sake get further involved. So you're sorry for her but with what you know about her now you'll be better off out of it. You've done more than enough already. If you go back to Meudon you'll be making a statement to her, taking a responsibility. I went out and ate at a brasserie on the corner of the Place des Ternes and then I went to the cinema for relief. In France, going to the cinema is still a valid intellectual activity; I felt better when I came out. It was dark by then and Paris had on its glare for the tourists, but I decided to go to bed.

There was a message waiting for me in the hotel pigeon-hole. A telephone call, no, three calls, all urgent. The last one was quite simple. It said: 'Tim, please come to Meudon as soon as you get this. Very urgent. Jacky.'

'What time did you get this?' I demanded of the porter.

He looked at it carefully. 'About, let me see, one hour ago. From a call-box, it was.' The Boiteaus had no phone in the house, I remembered that. 'She seemed agitated. Yes, it was before the man called to see you.'

'Man? A policeman? Called Dagallier?'

The porter grinned. 'No, monsieur, it was no policeman. A dark man, with hair en brosse. Black hair. Glasses. Thick eyebrows. Like this.' He drew his finger across his own eyebrows to emphasize the heavy nature of the hair.

'He came here?'

'About half an hour ago. I told him you were out. You had calls waiting in your pigeonhole. Monsieur, your key—'

But I was running by then, out of the door and up the street to the taxi rank at the top, facing the Etoile.

CHAPTER 20

Some instinct made me pay off the taxi at the corner of the Rue Babie and the main, downward Avenue Jacqueminot. It was late and dark. As I walked past the deserted lot at No. 8, with its outgrown limes and intrusive chestnut shoots spearing the rustling weeds, I felt a shiver of apprehension. It was there, somewhere in that deserted garden, that the start of this long and strange chase had been instigated; its brooding, dark calm seemed to await the outcome in sombre silence.

There was no policeman outside the Boiteaus' house. The shuttered windows at the front showed an occasional chink of light from within and assuaged my immediate stab of fear by suggesting that he was inside, sharing a drink or a coffee. The gate was closed but not latched, so it swung open with ease, silently, allowing me to reach the front door in three quick strides. I was brought up sharply at its weathered surface by the memory of the last time I had seen it, half-open, with Falco's black eyebrows scowling out of the gap between it and the jamb. I was about to knock when, to my left, towards the corner of the house, I saw a glint of light on a gendarme's hat, lying peak upwards on the path leading to the back garden. The hair on the back of my neck prickled hedgehog-sharp and my legs suddenly seemed quite inadequate for my weight. The street was quiet, suburban, deserted. How long would it take me to run and get help? The gendarmerie was on the other side of town; to reach a telephone would involve knocking on doors, delays, explanations. What might have happened by the time I got back with help? From inside I heard the distinctive sound of a piece of furniture being moved, shoved along the floor. Then there was a slap; a sharp crack of flesh being hit, hard.

That did it. I strode round the side of the house as quietly as I could, along the same path round the two right-angles I had trod the time before. This time the kitchen door was locked. I was shut out.

'*Non! Jamais!*' The distant voice was high, shrill, terrified. '*Ah! Non! Jamais!*'

The kitchen windows were the long, double type, with sills three feet from the ground. One opened above a draining-board, cluttered with pots and pans. The other had a table under it, a simple strong deal table that they probably ate off in normal circumstances. The catches holding the hinged windows were the old simple latch type and the cheap frames had no overlapping moulding. My penknife went into the join below the latch and, with an upward slide, lifted it easily. I hopped on to the sill, crossed the table and eased myself carefully to the floor before crossing to the hall. I nearly trod on the still form of the unconscious gendarme, tied and gagged where he lay against the stairs.

They were in the front room. Jacky Boiteau sat on the sofa, face marked by red blotches. The miserable-looking scruffy type I had hit before held her arms behind her.

'*Où est-il?*' From behind the living-room door, out of my sight, Falco's dread voice grated.

She shook her head dumbly. Her eyes stared behind the door in terrified fascination. I crept back into the kitchen to look for a weapon and decided on a hefty white china rolling-pin. Carefully I eased back into the hall.

The scruff let go of her arms and pulled out a broad, thin knife with a blade about six inches long. He grinned at the figure behind the door as he held it close to the girl's ear.

'Let me persuade her,' he said.

I heard Falco cross the room to his left. Suddenly he appeared, on the far side, near a single chair. He shook his head with a grin and took off his jacket, hanging it carefully over the chair back. In his shirtsleeves he looked even more menacing, stripped for action. He crossed back to the girl.

'*Jamais? Eh, bien, maintenant on va s'amuser avec toi.*' He smiled as he spoke, a meaning smile of physical intent. '*Après on verra si tu veux chanter.*'

I knew what the French verb *s'amuser* is used for; I didn't need reminding. He reached down and tore her printed cotton dress centrally, splitting it outwards as he pushed her back on to the sofa. It was time to move.

The scruff was still holding the knife close to Jacky's ear and the side of her neck as Falco pushed her backwards, tearing powerfully at the thin material. Bare flesh and white underwear gleamed under his intent, half-smiling face as he got her horizontal. I couldn't see the scruff's expression as I hit him behind the ear with the china rolling-pin, which promptly broke into four pieces, but I bet it was surprised. He pitched forward on to the girl and Falco, knocking him sideways off the settee on to all fours, so I kicked him, up and under, into the stomach, leaving the scruff to digest what I thought was a knock-out blow.

It was a mistake. Falco took the kick in the stomach with a tremendously satisfying grunt of pain but grabbed at my foot as I withdrew it, swinging me off balance. I managed to get away from his grasp but I was off kilter and staggered a pace back to meet the wall behind me and steady myself. By that time he was on his feet, bent double, coming at me like a battering ram. I sidestepped, chopping at his neck, and he rammed the wall. His knees buckled. Jacky let out a terrific scream.

Coming off the sofa with his knife in his hand was the scruff, quite clearly overjoyed at the prospect of evening up the score. She half stood up, her defenceless flesh exposed, and grabbed his arm in a silly attempt to deter him. He turned, shook free the arm and hit her a hard backhander, staggering her across the room to tangle with the single chair bearing Falco's jacket. Her legs gone, she tipped over the chair and collapsed into the corner with a splintering crash. Falco hit me on the side of the head as my attention faltered.

The only chance I had was that, in a small room, there might not be enough space for them both to attack me at once. I hit Falco back hard, keeping out of his grasp—the last thing I wanted was a clinch—and stepped back a pace to kick him on the kneecap, seeing the scruff's knife flash out of the corner of my eye. Falco hopped back on one leg and I just had time to put out an arm as the knife stabbed in at my ribs. It was a lucky break; I missed the scruff's wrist but I turned the knife arm outwards so that the blade flashed by an inch from my chest. As his weight followed the knife-swing he came colliding into me and I turned him, so that Falco hit him hard in the kidneys instead of getting me in the stomach. He gave out a scream of pain, but the impact pushed the two of us close together and I had trouble getting free of him as Falco closed again.

I managed to ward off a chop to the neck and another at my guts but to do it I had to move, so that the scruff somehow got behind me. Suddenly my luck had run out; I was facing Falco, whose face cracked into a triumphant grin, and the scruff was behind me, preparing for his doubtless favourite knife-thrust at my back. If I turned, Falco would get me; if I didn't, the scruff would.

That was when the gun went off.

At the time, it seemed like an explosion of major dimensions. The blast, in the confined room, seemed ear-splitting, stunning. There was a spatter, a gasp, then another explosion. Falco, still facing me, swore, not loudly, but the *merde!* of a man lost. I heard a thud; it was the knife, dropping.

Bang! Blood and tissue spattered the wall to my right. Jacky was sitting in the corner, her knees up. Both hands held the huge automatic, steadied in the groove made by the knees clamped together. The body of the scruff, hit a third time as it smacked into the wall, slid to the meagre carpet. Falco held up his arm in a gesture of restraint, almost of supplication, as his mind took in the fact that, in hanging up his jacket with his gun in it before his intention to amuse himself with a stripped-off Jacky, he had lost the game. Her face, distorted with terror and hatred, held no hope for him.

'*Non! Attendez—*'

Crash! It was no good; her panic made it worse. She pulled and pulled at the trigger, smashing the ear-splitting bullets across the room, ignoring my shouts of 'Stop, Jacky, its enough, enough, he's dead now, stop it,' as though wanting to blot out every memory of every man, every humiliation and exploitation, pumping away wildly so that

I feared, for some moments, that she would swing the barrel towards me too. But then the hammer clicked on the mercifully empty chamber and we were left, staring at each other in horror and gratitude across the blood-splashed, cordite-stinking room.

CHAPTER 21

Dagallier came into the kitchen, where I was restoring myself with one-star cooking brandy and gave me a disapproving stare. Jacky Boiteau, covered in a large blanket I had found upstairs, still shivered with shock. Her teeth chattered on the rim of the glass I had given her.

'Patients in shock,' he said severely, 'should not be given alcohol.'

'Sez you.'

'This is a complex matter and very grave. It will take a long time to reach satisfactory explanations; you will appear before an examining magistrate, do you realize that?'

'Oh yes; I read Inspector Maigret stories too.'

His disapproval deepened.

'Flippancy is not required. The humoristic point of view from which the English obtain their attitude to life will not go down well. On the other hand, my men—'

His men were moving about the hall and front room, taking photographs, moving things. The trussed, recumbent gendarme had been freed and carried away, still half-conscious. Having got Jacky out of the gore-spattered room I had not ventured back; I considered my role in calling the police to be quite sufficient. The street outside was packed with vehicles, people, flashing lights.

'—my men are, in their way, impressed. Particularly in view of the likely death of their comrade, who would have been despatched without compunction after the girl and you, once the objective was achieved. So I am also very glad, but I feel you have concealed matters from me and I must ask you to accompany me. Mlle Boiteau will need some clothes; I will arrange it.'

She gazed at him with a little more composure and nodded. 'Upstairs. The room on the left. My coat, something to—'She kept the blanket closed, but looked at me hopefully, glancing from the letters I had carefully smoothed on to the kitchen table. A man was despatched upstairs.

'Talking of the objective,' I said to Dagallier, 'I think we should achieve that, for safekeeping, before we leave.'

'*Comment?*'

There had been time, before they all arrived, for the half-hysterical Jacky to show me the letters she had been given that afternoon, the letters which prompted her to ring me so urgently. I handed Dagallier the first letter, holding it carefully at the edges, and cautioned him. 'This is an historical document. It will also be needed legally, to establish title. Be very careful. It was written by Gwen John.'

He flashed a policeman's glance at me and began to read the almost illegible scrawl, carefully but jerkily set out by a near-hermit who had lived, lonely and careless of health or food, by herself for two or three years. It was in French, addressed to Madame Boiteau. He muttered his way through the introduction and began to mouth the second paragraph.

It is clear that Paris is once again likely to be invaded and I cannot face a repeat of the terrible siege of the years of the 1914–18 war. Good Madame Roche opposite has promised to look after most of my cats but you know that there are three, all offspring of G----s, that she refuses to take because of their wildness and attacks on birds. You and I have always loved cats and I will be eternally grateful to you for caring for them with the love I know you feel. Who knows how long you will have them?

This is a terrible time. I hope they will be good and bring
you consolation as they and the Good Lord have done
to me. If I do not return I know they will be in safe
hands.

One more thing; I also pass the box to you for safekeeping with this note for you in case of difficulties. I
have had it for thirty-four years, since I accepted it from
him to prevent that woman from getting it.

Dagallier looked up at me. 'That woman?'
'I think she meant the Duchesse de Choiseul. When
the Duchesse took over in Rodin's affections she started
appropriating all sorts of his gear. There was a similar
outbreak when he was dying in 1917, in the Biron. Women
claiming to be lifelong mistresses fought each other for
sculptures and removed them. I don't believe Gwen John
would ever have stooped to that. And thirty-four years; that
means that she had it from 1905. This note was written in
September 1939.'

He looked at me thoughtfully before reading the valedic-
tory remarks at the end.

If anything happens to me I leave the box and its contents
for you to keep, like the cats. I have never told anyone
about it; I was his true wife; it is not suitable for my
family. It does not matter now what—

'I cannot read the rest.' He looked at me curiously. 'Cats
and a box? Cats I have seen, descendants I presume, but a
box?'

Jacky cleared her throat as she passed him the other
letter. 'Because my aunt died, this was given to me today
via a public notary. She had no money but she has left me
this house, the letter and a box.'

Dagallier took it, putting the Gwen John note down with
care. He read the next letter, with its clearer hand, much

more rapidly and silently, but I could feel the words passing into his brain as he scanned them.

'*Ma chère Jacqueline*—'

A preamble explaining about the will leaving the house to her and expressing the love the aunt had felt for her niece, the hole that she had filled in her life, giving it purpose and meaning. If only pauvre Mlle John had had someone like her to care for and love perhaps she would not have been so strange, so reclusive and lonely. The letter from Mlle John enclosed was left with three cats and a box when she left the Rue Babie in the first days of September 1939 to avoid the oncoming Germans. Madame Boiteau kept both carefully all through the war and for long afterwards, when her own terrible loss had made the departure and reported death of Mlle John fade into insignificance.

Jacky wept, knowing what he was reading, even though she had been through the letter several times already. I gave her my handkerchief and Dagallier flashed me a glance as he asked, 'What happened to her?'

'Gwen John? She got off the train at Dieppe and collapsed. She had no luggage. They took her to a hospice as a pauper and a vagrant and she died there. No one knows where she's buried.'

He read on, aloud this time.

When I finally realized that she would never come back and her family had cleared the shed across the road and sold it, I took out the box. It was, by this time, the nineteen-fifties and no one had heard of poor Mlle John. Although I had buried the box in the garden, to keep it safe, it was not much deteriorated. Inside was a figure; even after so many years I could recognize the face, so thin and pinched, of Mlle John. I did not know what it was worth or what to do with it, so I hid it again for the future. And then you came to me and filled my life with hope and happiness, even though it came through the

terrible loss of my dear nephew and his wife. The little
figure was somehow not really mine; I felt like the curator
of it, waiting for the right person to come and claim it.
When I die, you must have it and decide what to do with
it, unless, that is, there is someone or some organization
to whom it should really belong. I have been to the Musée
Rodin and to the Villa des Brillants here in Meudon.
They have so much already and this is a modest thing
compared to their superlative bronzes and marbles. Perhaps one day a suitable new collection should have it.

Dagallier's eyes came up over the top of the letter and
met mine.

'You've seen what she wrote to me,' I said, uncomfortably.
'I think she intended to interview me to see if we were
suitable.'

He tapped gently on the letter as he looked at me. 'Someone else got to know about it. Who, and how? We cannot,
now, ask the gentlemen in the front room to answer those
questions.'

'I have an idea,' I said, 'but very circumstantial. Let's find
the figure first. Then you can go through all the evidence.'

He looked back down at the letter and read on.

In the meantime I have kept the figure in its box. Not in
the ground any more, for fear of rot. At the back of the
coal shed, outside, there is a wooden battening to protect
the wall from the shovel. Behind that, in a cavity, you
will find the box.

'Legrand!' shouted Dagallier at one of his men in the hall.
'*Ici!*'

'You'll need a shovel,' I said. 'There's a couple of
hundredweight piled up against it.'

Dagallier got two men and made them illuminate the
little shed in the back yard while Legrand dug it out. When

he began to fumble at the battening at the back I issued a caution.

'If it's not bronze or marble, you'd better be careful. It may be fragile; if it's plaster it's probably pretty far gone, crumbled.'

But they were careful, gentle even, Frenchmen with their faces intent and excited, proud of themselves and their presence there. They bore the oblong hardwood box, about two feet long and eighteen inches high, tenderly into the kitchen and put it on the table. Then they looked at Jacky and Dagallier and me.

'You'd better open it,' Dagallier said to me. 'You're the art expert.'

Jacky nodded her acceptance, looking at me in fearful anticipation. 'Go on, Tim. I can't bear it. Open it, for God's sake.'

The hardwood was that cheap mahogany or baywood that you get in late nineteenth- and early twentieth-century furniture. I penknifed the top open carefully and found the box to be full of straw stuffing, carefully packed round the little statue inside. My fingers shook a bit as I pulled out the packing at the sides and got a grip on the figure, a greyish-salmon in colour, with a deeper red in the creases. I stood it upright on the table in that bare kitchen; a thing of beauty is a joy forever—that really is Keats, as a matter of fact.

'It's her all right. But she's the wrong way round—wait a minute, no she's not. Yes she is. And she's draped, like the plaster in the photograph.'

There was no mistaking the attitude and the face, with its narrow chin and open mouth, exactly like the one in the Musée Rodin. But this was a mirror image; she was posed the other way, right leg up instead of left, like a reversed photograph. And the lower limbs were draped in cloth folds.

'What is it?' Jacky's voice had an hysterical edge to it. 'What is it made of?'

'Oh.' I jerked my thoughts back from a sketch I had seen in one of my stolen books. 'Sorry. It's terra cotta. Not plaster. Terra cotta.'

'Is that no good?'

'As a matter of fact,' I said, and I meant it, 'I almost prefer it. It isn't as highly finished or sophisticated as bronze or marble but it's more like the original clay. Well, it is clay really, but it's been fired. I've always thought it a very warm and interesting medium. And look how accurately it can be sculpted, just like the other materials. Rodin produced quite a lot of things in terra cotta; he even did one or two in Sèvres pottery, which slightly misled me.'

'What did you mean—it's the wrong way round?'

'I meant that the piece is posed the reverse to the one we've known up to now. But you see it is entirely possible that Rodin did intend at one time for the monument to Whistler to have him up on a plinth, in robes, surrounded by four muses, looking up at him. The one in the Musée Rodin is the only one we've known up to now. This must have been meant to be one of the others or some other part of the study. It actually is much more like the one in his sketch of Gwen John posing early on, which *is* the reverse of the one in the Musée Rodin. It's really very exciting. In fact, it's a tremendous find.'

Relief and hope dawned across her face as she glanced from me to Dagallier, the flushed, excited, pleased policemen and back to me again. 'Oh Tim, you are so clever! Do you mean it may be worth something after all? Is it valuable?'

'I think,' I said, carefully turning the pink figure round on the kitchen table, 'that subject to the clearance of title and any requirements of the French authorities, of course, we would be prepared to give you a suitably substantial sum for it. Enough to keep you off the—I mean, enough to keep the wolf away from the door for some considerable time.'

CHAPTER 22

The sun was bright and hot on the bridge at Branne this time. It made the fast water sparkle beneath me on its way to join the Garonne. Through Peyroulas I turned left, up the tiny minor road towards St Hippolyte before sorting out the way around the lanes to the château. The hot sunshine struck my body as I got out on to the gravel in front of the warm stone house and I stretched stiffly, enjoying the relief. On the slopes amid the neat formal rows of vines, waist high, figures moved in slow rhythms of work, away from the puttering tractor perched high above the lines on its special chassis. As I watched, a woman stood upright to ease her back and a child, running by, stopped to raise its arms and be hoisted, laughing, on to her hip. A stooped man nearby straightened himself too, and exchanged words I could not hear with the woman as they stood isolated among the vines in the rolling slopes, with the blue haze of the Dordogne river plain behind.

'Idealized figures in an idealized landscape,' I said out loud, as Henry Dechavanne, in a grey mohair lightweight suit, came crunching across the gravel towards me.

'Mr Simpson? Good morning. I'm afraid I did not catch your remark. I can not say that this is an unexpected pleasure because Sir Richard has contacted me and advised me that you might visit but not, apparently, with his blessing?'

His face looked straight into mine, the eyes unblinking but guarded, searching my own countenance for emotional clues. I put my arms, folded in front of me, on the car roof, cooled by the wind of travel, and rested my chin on them, legs braced backwards to ease the knees as I looked at him without shaking hands in any sort of greeting.

'Idealized figures in an idealized landscape,' I said again, so that he could hear this time. 'It's what he painted, isn't it?'

His forehead furrowed, a quick reflex, blinking the eyes. 'Who?' he asked, curiously.

'Puvis de Chavannes. Little known in England but an influential artist. On people like Augustus John, who tried that type of painting and even, partly, on Picasso. It's amazing how small the world of art can be. Rodin, for example, knew Whistler although he didn't feel any particular warmth for him. Rodin was chosen to work on his monument. In working on it he in turn chose by pure chance an ex-pupil of Whistler's called Gwen John. Her brother Augustus also knew Whistler and was influenced by Puvis de Chavannes, who was in turn a close friend of Rodin's. Just like *La Ronde*, isn't it? The world is a very small place sometimes, quite frightening.'

'You think so? I have the impression that you are not easily frightened.'

'Oh? No, not usually. Do you think he had any more children? Rodin, I mean.'

His brow furrowed again. 'There was just one. Beuret. Auguste Beuret, son of his mistress, Rose, the one he finally married.'

'Beuret was backward, or difficult. Sir Richard thinks that Rodin might have had syphilis and been treated with mercury. It does seem odd that there were no more children. Augustus John had lots of them.'

The brown eyebrows shot up, widening the blue eyes. 'Does Richard think that? He belongs to another, rather older generation.' He smiled confidentially at me. 'Perhaps his parents warned him of such things rather strongly when he was young. I am sure that it was not so. Rodin lived a long life, physically powerful and with a clear, fine mind right up to the end. Everything about him was well documented.'

'So I believe. But it does seem curious. Talking of documentation, I had forgotten until recently how close a friend of Rodin's Puvis de Chavannes was. Very close. In fact, Rodin was very upset when Puvis didn't like the bust that Rodin had produced of him in marble.'

'Have you come here to lecture me on French art history, Mr Simpson?'

'Oh no. I just wanted to clear my thoughts. You see, it was that background that convinced me, in the end, of how very avidly a man descended from Puvis de Chavannes would want to own a work by Rodin of a Welsh model. Particularly a rapacious collector of Sèvres, where Rodin worked between 1878 and 1882. But much more particularly a man whose father was a descendant of Puvis and whose mother came from Wales. From Carmarthen, appropriately enough. Did she call you Henry after Henry Tudor?'

He stared fixedly at me, the face unchanged but still, with the control of a poker player or of a man whose life had been spent in protracted commercial negotiations needing great patience, cunning, hidden thought. I turned away from the stare to look away out over the landscape where the woman still stood with the laughing child on her hip and another child now beside her, with the man nearby watching the group good-humouredly. Dechavanne spoke from behind me, his voice guarded.

'It is getting very hot out here. For an Englishman, with no protective hat, it could be injurious to health. Indeed, it could affect one's judgement. May I suggest that we go inside, Mr Simpson, to my study, and take a little refreshment?'

'OK. Thank you.'

We walked beside each other across the crunching gravel without speaking. At the big front doors a woman servant opened up for us with a respectful nod and we passed through into the high, cool hall. Dechavanne led the way to his study, warm in tone but still airy, where a bottle stood open on a silver tray, flanked by two glasses.

'I am expecting a *négociant* from Libourne a little later,' he said. 'I opened a bottle of the '71 for him to try but I have more in reserve. Would you like to try a glass too, or would you prefer coffee?'

'Thank you, no coffee. I would love to try a glass.'

He smiled. 'At least you have not been affected by your country's deplorable laws on the availability of alcohol, Mr Simpson. Forgive me; I do not mean to be condescending. From the way you speak French and from Sir Richard's remarks about your South American background, I should have expected a more—international, should I say?— approach to a drink anyway.' He poured a glass carefully.

The claret was superb, filling my mouth with warmth, fruit and richness. I must have looked impressed for he smiled at me again.

'I hope you will not take it amiss, but you drink a little too quickly. To savour the wine you should have sniffed a little more, held it in your mouth longer and sipped a little less quantity rather than swallowing that way.'

I grinned. 'Oh, no offence taken. I know I'm a very bad drinker of wine generally. I quaff too much. It comes of swigging beer in pubs during my extreme youth; somehow the intake of alcohol becomes associated with the quenching of thirst rather than appreciation. That and the rather different attitude they have to wine down round the River Plate probably accounts for it.'

There, I thought, you know now that it wasn't nerves. I put the glass down and he waited, watching me.

'It was the Sèvres that threw me for a bit,' I said. 'I wasn't sure whether the piece that poor Madame Boiteau possessed was a piece of Sèvres by Rodin or at least a design of his. It would have accounted for your criminally voracious pursuit of it. But Rodin left Sèvres in 1882 and he didn't meet Gwen John until 1904, twenty years later. It was most unlikely, even though his assistant, Desbois, took over his post at Sèvres. The last thing I could come across that Rodin did in Sèvres pottery was the bust of Carrière-Belleuse and that was way back. The only pointer was your violently acquisitive collector's urge; an interesting characteristic which leads many to ruthless activities. I imagine that you collect Sèvres from the great eighteenth-century period, anyway, not from the debased late nineteenth?'

He didn't answer; his face was set into an expression of intense attention, like a man listening to an important broadcast which might affect his course of action in some way, so I went on.

'Then there was the question of your descent, which you laughingly denied when I first asked you. But your face went very still when I mentioned the influence of Puvis on Augustus John. That and Puvis' close relationship with Rodin were, shall we say, straws in the wind. Dechavanne and de Chavannes must be linked in some way, even if only in your family's legends. I'm not a genealogist and I didn't have enough time in Paris to get very far with that line of inquiry. You said your mother was English. The French word Anglais or Anglaise is used loosely to cover everyone in Britain usually, although you are more circumspect about. recognizing the Scottish, who are your old allies against the English common enemy. But Welsh—Pays de Galles—not so prominently, although you knew the difference full well. The records in France and papers generally say your mother came from London, which at the time of her marriage to your father was true. She went to London University to read law. Rather unusual for a woman at the time; she must have been very clever.'

'She was.'

'Quite the home town success story really, a Carmarthen girl getting a scholarship in London in the late Twenties, but not unheard-of. She never practised; I assume she met your father—in London?'

'No, in Paris, on a cultural visit.' His voice was gentler now, more thoughtful.

'Ah. Well, anyway, a little research, Somerset House, the usual sources I'm afraid, very dull and boring, but they record her birth in Carmarthen.'

'You are very thorough, Mr Simpson.'

'Well, it's my job, you see, like a reflex action. You concealed the fact from Sir Richard presumably because he might have thought that your choice was influenced by emotion rather than commercial judgement. Indeed, there was no need particularly for anyone to know. Carmarthen suited you for other reasons too. But then the news about the Rodin, the Gwen Rodin as I call it, sentimentally or emotionally was too much for you. A voracious collector faced with the existence of a really appropriate item, an obsessive item. You couldn't bear to sit back and let stuffy old White's Bank pick it up for its Art Fund, lost to you forever. You sent that lethal thug Falco to get it; quite a cheap way of acquiring it, really. And you sent him to ransack my rooms when you failed in the Rue Babie. You told him to take anything connected with Rodin and Gwen John. He only got my books—not a great deal of help, I imagine, so you kept him on my trail as well as the Boiteaus'.'

He scowled fiercely. 'You are suggesting that I was involved in some criminally violent theft? Ridiculous; for a start, I could not have known about this piece.'

'Oh yes you could! Sir Richard told you, I bet! He couldn't keep it to himself, could he? You and he were so close about the project; it was an all-pervading obsession of his. What pleasure he must have taken in telling you how clever, how suitable a decoration to the foyer of the new building it would be! An almost local Welsh artist lady sculpted by a famous Frenchman, Rodin no less. Little did Sir Richard know how suitable it was, to you. I had told him the name: Boiteau, Rue Babie. He blurted it out to you, I bet.'

'He certainly did not! You have no evidence whatsoever,

no possible means of substantiating these absurd, insulting and preposterous claims!'

'No, none.'

His head, which had lowered itself like a bull's preparing for a charge, came up to the vertical again. The neck and jaw muscles, tensed in bunches, relaxed. He even sat up straighter, higher, the pose of a man reaching a dominant position, looking down at his adversaries.

'I believe that you knew Falco from work done for you in Quebec; Montreal, perhaps, or Victoriaville? I have little doubt that there is no documentary evidence to link you, and Falco is dead, so there will be no comeback from that source as I am sure you know. But I know, and Sir Richard knows, that we didn't send Falco to attack Madame Boiteau and get the little statue. So the finger points at you. The police here in France find that a very interesting matter; there's an inspector in Meudon who is most interested in you, now.'

'Ridiculous, circumstantial evidence!'

'Indeed. But Sir Richard told you, in a fit of enthusiasm about the tissue project, which was his great private crusade into modern times on behalf of the Bank. Pity, really, because it will not now take place. Not with White's participation, anyway.'

His face changed. 'Why not?'

'Because Jeremy was always against it and I am now against it and I'm afraid that the evidence will prevent Sir Richard from supporting it even if he were probably not now against it also.'

'Evidence? What do you mean?'

I took another swallow of the claret. 'You simply can't help it, can you? Cheating is a way of life to you. The equipment prices for the factory which have been presented to the Welsh authorities are hideously overloaded; thirty per cent up. Nearly a million pounds. Which your Italian equipment friends would pay into an account of your choosing, in Switzerland or Jersey or Bermuda or wherever. So it doesn't really matter that much whether the project would be successful or not because you'd be a million up to start with. The venture might be successful, though; who knows? It's a gamble. A good gamble for you, with a million start, but not for White's.'

He got up. 'If the Italians have tried to profiteer on us it will be thoroughly investigated! There is alternative equipment available. I shall take this up personally!'

'Oh yes. Now. Now that the discovery has been made. But it reflects badly on your competence even if not directly on your honesty. I find it more interesting that you should try to perpetuate your mother's memory by instigating a fraud in her home town.'

'It is not a fraud! The project is perfectly viable!'

'Possibly. But you were going to pocket nearly a million pounds without your partners knowing. I wonder what she would have thought of that?'

He stared at me. Intensity of an indefinable sort suffused his face. Suddenly he smiled, grimly. 'She would have enjoyed the joke. Particularly since the money would have come from EEC funds, which are one of the biggest frauds of all. Like Gwen John, she left Wales in her twenties and she never went back. She made France her home and she became French. She died here. She despised the stifling atmosphere of Carmarthen just as much as the Johns did of Tenby. They all left the place. She would have enjoyed the joke.'

'So you could play it both ways. If the project were successful you could reveal what a benefactor you'd been to your maternal home town. If it weren't you could pocket your million and smile to yourself and your mother's memory. Quite a nice two-sided game to play.'

'The dry-forming project is not a game to me. I am committed to it.'

'So why let White's in on the act? If it's such a winner,

a man like you would keep it to himself. Anglo-French concordats mean nothing to you. No, I suspect that White's were to be a form of insurance; if you were successful you'd take the benefits; if not, then White's would stand a lot of the losses. There's nothing like having a gullible partner to lean on, as everyone in the art trade knows.'

'Sir Richard will be interested to hear your assessment of him when we next meet. You do not know the full extent of his involvement, do you, Mr Simpson?'

'Oh, Sir Richard has been culpable, but not of collusion in your fraud; don't try to infer that. Apart from the lack of disclosure to his Board his main dereliction has been a lack of judgement. It happens to people looking for schemes to fit their ideals. In a way, Monsieur Dechavanne, you appeared to Sir Richard as an ideal figure in an ideal landscape. Whereas it only needed a realist to look at you.'

He glared at me for a moment, his whole large frame tensed as though he was contemplating a physical attack. Then he walked carefully round to my side of the table. His expression changed again, as though a shutter had snapped, closing off a compartment. The look was shrewd, accepting, as if to cut a loss and move on to the next, prepared position.

'Another glass?'

'Thank you, yes.'

He poured it carefully and walked to the long window which gave a view out over the landscape.

'White's must pay you a great deal, Mr Simpson. At the moment. One wonders from Sir Richard's tone just how long that will last.'

I didn't reply. The glass was at my lips and I watched, irritated.

'Forgive me; I did not mean to pry. But here in France a man of your calibre and—resourcefulness—could expect to be highly rewarded. Our tax system, too, is more generous to the talented than yours.'

'I know.' I drank a mouthful of the wine. Calibre and

resourcefulness seemed to me to be an improvement on fieldcraft and tenacity.

'Your French is excellent. And, if I may say so, you have a certain style which would serve you well here.'

'Oh?'

'Mr Simpson, to my bank you would be worth at least one hundred thousand dollars. Many Englishmen of taste and energy find Bordeaux a very congenial city. Very Anglophile too.'

'Bordeaux is a handsome place. I've always admired it.'

'One hundred thousand dollars.'

'I'm afraid not. I already have questions of loyalty to resolve internally, without—'

'As a joining fee, of course. Paid wherever you like. Then an annual salary of the same amount.'

I got up, leaving the rest of the wine in the glass. 'Monsieur Dechavanne, I regret to confess that you have shown me a considerable temptation, which shows what small beer I must seem to you. I am not anxious to become Falco's replacement, quite apart from the question of justice for poor Madame Boiteau and the fraud you attempted to perpetrate. I did say that the world of art is frighteningly small. So is the world of banking. Nothing that you could ever sue for will be said or written but I fancy that the word will get around.'

He laughed, openly. 'You threaten me with private sanctions? On all this circumstantial evidence? I had thought that you were more intelligent.'

'Oh, I agree, plenty of finance people in France would be amused at your taking stuffy old White's for a ride. They'd be just like the art trade; if you're a professional you should know a fake when you see one. *Caveat emptor*. But—'

'But nothing, my dear Mr Tim Simpson! Money always talks. People deal with others as they find them, provided they are not convicted criminals. Each project, each deal, stands or falls on its own merits, the way the cards are received and played. The French have no illusions about things like that, their sang-froid makes them realistic, logical, hard-headed businessmen, prepared to deal with anyone. As the English used to be.'

'Now who's talking history, or their version of it?'

He smiled. 'Excuse me. But my offer still stands. You are a very useful professional.'

'No, thank you all the same. I must leave.'

'Pity. I will see you to your car.'

He walked outside with me, carefully, over the gravel expanse above the rolling vine-lined fields facing the spread river plain. His face betrayed nerves, cautiously held back, but he looked at me quizzically, even humorously.

'No drama, Mr Simpson? No punch on the jaw? No boy scout, righteous violence? Richard said that there was an element of the boy scout in you, which made me underestimate you. I would not do so now.'

My face twitched. 'No. No drama. Nor you, either? No gunman on the roof? No poison in the wine?'

He laughed outright. 'Do you think I would risk losing one of my best *négociants*? No, not me either. Look—look out over the landscape: the workers are about their business again. The woman no longer stands with the child on her hip, like an Ida or a Dorelia to be painted by Augustus. Or Puvis. The idealized figures are no longer in the idealized landscape; it was a transitory image. They are back at work, as we all have to be. For as much as we can gain. My offer still stands.'

He gave a half-gesture of farewell and left me at the car. As he walked away he turned just once more to look back. His face in the bright sun was dark, shadowed, inward, so that when I tried to recall it later, all I could see in my mind's eye were the smudges cast by the protuberances of nose, eyebrows, jaw. Yet it was a lividly sunny day and the view carried for miles. I sensed the direction of his gaze as it shifted out beyond Castillon and he spoke for the last time.

'Old Sir Richard's iron madonna is a monument to an incompetent, violent old man whose supporters lost their lives from his misjudgement. I hope you will have the sense to absorb its lesson correctly.'

I had no time to reply. As he spoke a car came up the long drive and he moved to meet it as it pulled to a halt at the bottom of the entrance steps. He walked over and clapped the arriving *négociant* on the back as he got out of the car, putting an arm around his shoulders as they walked together up the wide stone staircase flanked by the urns.

He didn't look back again.

CHAPTER 23

'Fifty thousand?' queried Jeremy, the morning after Sir Richard's resignation. 'Do we really have to pay that much?'

'Tut, tut, Jeremy,' I said, reclining in his office easy chair. 'City mendacity is starting to affect you already.'

He gave me a mock scowl as Mary Waller smiled. 'You're sure it is genuine, Tim?'

'The experts all say so. You can check terra cotta for age by analysis and there are the accompanying documents. An important find. Articles will be written. Experts will hold forth. Pontiffs will pontificate. The Art Fund will obtain great prestige. The National Museum of Wales will grind its teeth in jealous rage. Isn't that what we all want? Or is it all too minor a business now?'

He ignored the leading question. 'It seems extraordinary that it hasn't come to light until now.'

'In her room in the Terre Neuve in Meudon, before she moved to the Babie, Gwen John had rows of unfinished canvases, rotting, some of them. No one knows what happened to those, either. I heard a story of a man who had a head of Balzac by Rodin stuck in his garden all through the war. You never can tell what might come to light. It's what makes the art market what it is.'

'The girl—Jacqueline Boiteau—has proper title to it?'

'Yes. It's obviously unique, Jeremy. The French authorities are being very cheerful about it, treating it as a sort of cultural exchange, goodwill occasion, that sort of thing. No one will ever be told the full story, but at least Dechavanne didn't get it in exchange for a few thousand quid paid to a thug.'

'What a shit.' Jeremy's voice betrayed little emotion. 'What a filthy, conniving shit.'

'Not really. When a crocodile sees an inexperienced land animal entering the water it can't help itself assuming that dinner has arrived. English generals should not go into action in France without their armour on. Funny that Sir Richard didn't see the lesson of history that way.'

There was a silence. Mary Waller looked down at her hands.

'He won't be coming in again, ever?'

Jeremy shook his head. 'He resigned absolutely at the meeting yesterday. On generous terms, of course.'

'Of course.'

'Now, Tim.'

'Oh, don't get me wrong. I'm really quite sorry for him. I still think his heart was in the right place, even if his attitude and execution were appalling. Come on, Jeremy, out with it; who takes over?'

He sighed. 'You were right. It was too premature for me. They've put in a caretaker chairman. Lord Larkfield from the brokers. They've decided to approach Peter Lewis to see if they can get him back from Singapore as managing director. His children are of school age so he may want a spell back here after all. With his father-in-law gone and a decent salary package, most of it paid elsewhere, he might come.' He brightened up a bit. 'Still, it's one out of the way.

Leaves my other two cousins in a dominating position but at least old Richard's out of it.'

'God! We could go on like this for years.'

Mary Waller shook her head. 'Go on, Jeremy, tell him. By the way, Tim, we're official now, Jeremy and me.'

'Congratulations. I can kiss you now, can I?'

'Of course.'

And very agreeable too. After a suitable pause she said, 'Well, go on, Jeremy, tell him.'

He cleared his throat. 'Yes, well. We had a long discussion at the meeting about our management structure, as you can imagine. In view of the changing world, and all that. To cut it short, we're creating a new position, called Associate Director, for those who we think should play a more prominent role in the Bank's affairs.'

Without, I thought wrily, altering the composition of the Board itself or the retention of power by the family.

'Er, naturally you are one of the first we would put in this new important position, with all it implies. There will be three others.'

'I see. How kind.'

'Rubbish,' said Mary Waller. 'He can't do without you. And you'll be very good at it. You know you will.'

Jeremy grinned suddenly. 'You will accept, won't you? I made an awful fuss to get it through. I do have you to thank for so much, Tim.'

I laughed. 'In that case it would be churlish to refuse. On one condition, though.'

'What's that?'

'I have a week off before starting. I need a rest from all this excitement.'

'Done.'

They escorted me to the door promising that they'd send Jacky the draft for fifty thousand and I went downstairs, getting a wink from the old lag on the lift. The majordomo scuttled out of his office and did the equivalent of tugging a forelock as he signalled the lackey outside. News travels fast; they considered me to be one of them now, not just a temporary visitor.

'No, thanks, no taxi. I'll walk to the tube.' Was I really a member of the Bank now? Me? It seemed incredible to think of myself as belonging to this nest of gamesters. I walked away from the big Cuban mahogany doors down towards Gracechurch Street, that typically City thorough-fare to servitude for thousands of commuters who stream across the river to it in transpontine—George Melly adjec-tive—journeys from southern parts. The Underground station sign appeared in front of me, interrupting my thoughts: Monument.

Talbot's, Whistler's, Edwin John's and this one; odd how certain themes, once started, seem to pervade life for a bit.

CHAPTER 24

The sun was smiling on the Old Brompton Road as I strolled down its busy pavement to Onslow Gardens. The flat looked light and airy; I was admiring the flowered wallpaper and deciding where to put the hi-fi when the doorbell rang. I opened up and let Sue in.

'Goodness,' she said, standing uncertainly in her light summer suit with the slung satchell-handbag. 'This is a bit sparse. But it's nice and light, isn't it?'

'How did you find it?'

'Oh, Charles told me while I was at Christerby's yester-day. You are an awful liar, Tim.'

'Me? Why?'

'Charles told me how clever you've been. Over this Rodin of Gwen John. He's all agog about it. All the time I thought I was giving you the information; I bet you never even opened those papers?'

'Oh yes I did. They were invaluable, really. It was a great help to me. The information, I mean. I'd never have managed without it.'

Her lips twitched. 'You never were any good at lying. You didn't need me this time. Not at all.'

'Oh yes I did.'

She laughed. 'Now I know you're a cheat, Tim. Those papers were all about his plaster-casting technique and other technical details. They would have been no use to you at all.'

'Well, I—er—I did need—background, you know. Hope it hasn't upset Arthur or anything?'

She walked carefully along the back of the new settee, tracing a pattern with her finger. 'Tim, I've—I've broken off my engagement to Arthur. He just, well, he really wasn't suitable; too cautious, too studious for me. I suppose I'm still attracted by the real world. I, er, I wrote yesterday.' She glanced quickly at me and then down at the carpet.

Now who's lying, I thought; you shocking liar, Sue. There never was any Arthur; there couldn't have been. You invented him in some sort of war with me, as a defence system. But I said nothing. Let her win, a little voice said, go on, don't destroy the defence and trample on it, like you would have in the old days. Learn to let her win; start now.

So I said, 'I see,' dimly, as though digesting a new, completely unforeseen turn of events. 'I'm sorry. Sort of.'

'Are you really?'

'No.'

She laughed again, happily. 'What are you going to do now?'

'I've got a week off. To fix this place up.'

'That'll be nice.'

'Eh?'

She came round from behind the sofa then but she was always the English teacher-type and she said, after she'd put her arms around me and kissed me, 'This wallpaper is absolutely ghastly; we'll have to replace it. But don't worry, Tim: I'll choose the new paper and you can hang it. You'll be very good at that. As well.'

John Malcolm is a
founding member of the Antique Collectors'
Club and has authored several price guides to
antique furniture. He is the author of *A Back
Room in Somers Town* and *The Godwin Sideboard*.